The Cabals and the Naked Dance
(short stories)

Mnguember Vicky Sylvester

authorHOUSE®

AuthorHouse™
1663 Liberty Drive
Bloomington, IN 47403
www.authorhouse.com
Phone: 1 (800) 839-8640

This is a work of fiction. All of the characters, names, incidents,
organizations, and dialogue in this novel are either the products
of the author's imagination or are used fictitiously.

Published by AuthorHouse   11/19/2015

ISBN: 978-1-5049-5940-7 (sc)
ISBN: 978-1-5049-5941-4 (e)

Print information available on the last page.

Any people depicted in stock imagery provided by Thinkstock are models,
and such images are being used for illustrative purposes only.
Certain stock imagery © Thinkstock.

This book is printed on acid-free paper.

Because of the dynamic nature of the Internet, any web addresses or
links contained in this book may have changed since publication and
may no longer be valid. The views expressed in this work are solely those
of the author and do not necessarily reflect the views of the publisher,
and the publisher hereby disclaims any responsibility for them.

COMMENTARY

The stories are vivid in capturing contemporary issues, from the private to the public. Their exploration of life outside Nigeria, through the keen eyes of the ubiquitous female tourist, is remarkable. Perhaps most striking is the unique female angle that one gets in most of the stories. Gripping and bold, some of the stories bring us close to anxieities of girls and women trying hard to survive in a society that generally undermines their potentials. I'm particularly impressed that most of the female characters I encounter in the stories are strong and smart!

E.E. Sule

SCRAP

Attah was twenty four, tall, skimpily dressed, a heavily made up oval face illuminated by lights of the street along which she strutted, changing her steps with the light of an oncoming car. Her smooth skin and full breasts ballooned out of a tight fitting spaghetti blouse, a small jacket in her hand. Each time she turned under the third pole marking her operational zone of the space she walked, she would hiss loudly, hitching her expensive hand bag that matched her high, toe peeping comfortable shoes. On her side cars sped past, the drivers momentarily looking at her moderately large hips which she swayed proactively. She wriggled harder, knowing the effect on any male that would be watching each time she heard the sound of an approaching car. She knew the other girls were doing the same struthious movements but she was sure she had more to offer.

Attah was not unaware of the the dangers that came with what she was up to but she was a prayerful girl and was sure her guardian angel would not put her in the arms of a predator. She recalled the stories of Uche and Amaka who were taken to a hotel room and had waited for hours for a gentleman who liked to see girls play. They had thought this was better than a man who would refuse to use a condom and who could be ruthless in claiming his pay. They had been told by 9pm the man would be done with them as he had a wife who insisted on his coming home before she went to bed. It was midnight and they were thinking of just walking away before it was late to pick a taxi when the man who had contacted them opened the door only to appologise and tell them to be patient. Amaka had followed him to the door to tell him they would rather leave and come another day but the guy whom they hardly knew his name simply walked away into a room four doors down the corridor. Amaka turned to Uche and shook her head, 'I am going to talk to him. They can't keep us here like this,' and before Uche could say anything she was off.

Uche stood by the door unsure of what to do. Amaka could be unnecessarily stubborn. She needed the money tonight. Her brother needed school fees and if she did not get it fast he could be sent out ofschool. It happened last year, the second time since their mother died. She had gone to their uncle but his wife had sent them away. She had managed to take care of herself comfortably in the last two years, a year away to her graduation but now her thirteen year old brother had also become her responsibility. Two days earlier she had visited him with some provisions and he had told her the principal had announced at assembly that anyone whose fee was pending would be sent away this weekend. When Amaka told her of this meeting she had thanked God for His mercies. Their mother was not here but He was with them. She was still in deep thought when she saw Amaka speeding back like a rat from burning bush.

'Blood! Run,' and she had dashed after her. She could barely stay five steps behind Amaka as she ran past the reception to the gate. She headed for a cluster of hedges in front of a residential plot and stooped down holding on to each other. They bent low behind the hedge and waited. It was not long before a car came down the road with two men looking on each side of the road. It was not long before they returned slowing down near the hedge. A security man they had not seen walked towards the car and coughed,

'Any problem?' he asked but the car drove away. He turned to them,

'You see what this waka waka can do? Una no de hear word.' As he scolded them for roaming and how this could get them into trouble, the girls stood up and followed him to the security house where they huddled in a corner clutching their small purses. The security man walked away shaking his head.

'You are lucky today. Let this be a lesson', he said locking the gate.

The long wait came to an end as people hurried past with the Muslim call to prayer. It was not long before the prayers ended and the men talked quietly on their way home. The security man waited until they had gone into their homes and then opened the gate pulling a water hose after him. He stopped a taxi and called them out. They got into the car humbly thanking the man who had saved them. Amaka did not utter a word till they got out of the taxi. She looked around at the silent apartments as if saying a silent goodbye and headed for her door. Amaka threw her purse on the bed, pulled out a suit case and bag and began to throw in her belongings.

3

'You can go back to your hostel. I am not staying in this town any longer. Those people are ritual killers. You need to see what they had done to only God knows how many girls. Blood was everywhere and they were packing the chopped up bodies into black bags when I opened the door. For a while they didn't even know I was the one and were wondering if they could handle us at the time or give us another date.'

'What?' Attah shouted in horror.

'Yes. We were next in line,' Amaka said, pulling shirts from hanger to suit case.

'What do you want to put in this bag?' Attah jumped from the plastic chair she had slumped in. Amaka pointed to a basket containing a flask, cups and plates. Attah picked some news papers in a corner and began to wrap them. In about twenty minutes they were dragging the cases towards the road were they picked a taxi to the bus stop. They agreed it was not safe for Amaka to stay since the contact knew her. They did not know Uche. She was not even introduced to them. Attah had listened to the story and thanked God for deliverance and told Amaka to be careful.

As she walked away from the bus stop that morning she remembered Awanger's story which she had hardly believed then. Awanger had taken a ride and after the usual greetings and introductions, the man had told her she was lovely. He said he would like to see her again more intimately. Awange smiled politely and reminded him of her destination. The man bent over and opened the pigeonhole saying he would give her transport money to visit him the next day since she was now in a hurry. He used a face towel to pick a bunch of twenty thousand naira notes from the pigeonhole and then dropped the roll on the floor next to Awanger's feet. He then asked her to pick it. It was for her. Awanger had asked him why he would give her money on the floor and had refused to pick it. She had then told him to drop her as she had come to her destination. The man had stopped the car pleading with her to pick the money and had bent over, taken her hand as she stepped out of the car and tried to force it onto the notes but Awanger had pulled her hand away forcing his on the notes. To her shock the man had coiled and slumped on the passenger seat and slowly rolled into a slittering serpent.

Awanger had screamed and moved away from the door of the Peugeot drawing attention of the fruit and suya hawkers who ran towards the car, sized up the situation they seemed familiar with from their facial expressions. They opened the boot of the car, gathered the serpent into it and shut the boot. One of them turned to Awanger and asked her to move on. Awanger had rushed to her sister and recounted the story in tears. Within a few hours, the story was all over in the female hostel. Some of them had waved it away as an exaggerated tale. Attah knew the night had its dangers but one had to hope for the best to survive and she did not consider joining the robbery gangs or drug pushers a better deal. This was safer and she prayed she would not fall into the hands of ritualists, Attah thought as she walked towards the lighted pole.

On second thought Atttah decided to move a pole away from her designated place to the tree in the distance, away from the two figures behind her, each pacing within her territory. The night was worn and dawn was creeping upon her. She had to do something atrocious tonight. She made to return from the dark shade of the tree as a Mercedes Benz E-class drove up, slowing without coming to a standstill. She moved close up, pulled down her skirt to cover some thighs and slipped on her jacket using one hand to hold it to her half exposed breasts, 'Lift please,' she said with a difficult smile that showed her gap tooth.

'Where to?' came the face from the Benz

'Anywhere along IBB,' Attah answered with such relief that Anonde felt sorry for her believing he had guessed right, that the girl was stranded and one should not assume that a walking girl at a late hour was doing the night. He hardly looked at her heavy made up face, his mind on the rubbish thrown around the Jikwoi cemetery. No respect for the dead whose home, the cemetery was but littered by the living. Did they expect them, the dead to come out perhaps at night to clean up the mess? Well, he had heard it said that some people had powers to raise the dead to carry out farm or construction work for them at night. Perhaps no one with such powers lived around the Jikwoi cemetery. No one there thought of keeping the place clean and to think it could be their own home tomorrow, even today.

Nearby was a young man searching the garbage under the tree the girl had just walked away from. It was his presence that had sent Attah away from there. She could not be carefull enough with these thieves and rapists and messengers of ritualists who also walked the night in many disguises. She looked away from him with disgust. Anonde looked at the young man with sympathy. He was here like many others who left their home towns and villages in search of jobs. A friend had left and returned home once in a while looking wealthier, even buying a drink for a friend or two. It was enough reason for his friends and admirers to set forth. But many who came here were better off home where they had little or no money but some hand craft to perform, even the farm they no longer wanted and, of cause, food to eat and a warm place to sleep. At this hour! Anonde's heart went to the young man as he remembered many like him around a dump site where he had gone a week earlier with a director of the environmental protection agency. Anonde had taken a proposal from his organization in London, on a recycling project. It had been agreed that the enormous waste of plastics was good business in the country. He had spent two hours at the agency on what looked like a successful venture. The director, Dr Engr. Alh Mustafa seemed knowledgeable on the subject. He had noted that the collection would be a minor as lots of people were out there doing the unpaid work and his organization would simply mobilize them for a stipend in categorizing the dirt. The man searching the waste bin could be one of such people the engineer spoke about, Anonde concluded. Dr. Engr Alh Mustafa had driven Anonde to Gwagwalada where streets were densely populated with garbage. There were no refuse bins and one pile of garbage was oozing out smoke beside a muddy patch next to the Town Hall. That muddied heap was of no use and they had driven to the night market. Here at the night market was a mountain of good scrap and Anonde was pleased to hear the director say that was a day's rubbish. He had mentioned Nyanya, Mararaba, Karimo and Anonde had decided to check out the places on his own. The director was drawing a lot of attention away from their intentions by his presence. It was amazing the number of people that knew him and came to greet and then those who knew those who came to greet and had to give support by coming to greet. Some added a few more titles to the official ones the engineer had and it took quite some time to get over the greetings. Some of them asked after his home and then wife, children, mother and other relations known to the person greeting. Some commiserated with him again on the death of his father a year ago even though they were there at the funeral. A few others who heard of the loss for the first time expressed sympathy with him and said some prayers for the repose of the late man's soul. Anonde had found Karmo densely populated, poorly planned, muddy and water logged, with untarred roads, heaps of garbage with filthy stinking surroundings. He noted the garbage in some places filled with dead reptiles, used sanitary pads, nylon bags with human waste spilling out with scavenging maggots milling around. This would be of little use but he was sure the dump from the market at Ereke junction looked like good garbage. One of the men Anonde had spoken to at Karmo simply said he had to make do working next to the dirt because, 'We are being told that Abuja is for traders who can afford the high rent at Wuse or Area One. The task force has forced us out of Berger Junction and confiscated our goods even destroying some. Now they have sent some of the traders into theft and girls on the streets,' he concluded, looking at a little girl hurrying off to shool in muddied white stockings as if worried the girl would end up on the streets. Both men looked around from the umbrellas to the tables. From Karimo, the driver took Anonde to Angwa Tiv village. Though these people tried hard to keep the place clean it was difficult with the muddy open gutters which spilled its various contents on the patchy walkways around the houses. Several of the mud houses had collapsed the previous day from a heavy down pour and the occupants were seen talking in little groups here and there. From their discussions some had moved in with relatives or friends who were already crowded in small rooms. Others found places to keep their belongings different from the places they were sleeping. Some were talking of going back to their states until they could find an alternative. It sounded to Anonde like Abuja was a magnet to which these people were irresistibly drawn. Anonde found little to collect as the whole place was nothing but mud and dirt and young girls and boys milling around.

At this point Anonde looked sideways at Attah who looked ahead and appeared calm but whose mind seemed to in turmoil. And indeed Attah was troubled. She had come from the university to make some money that would see her through the week and if she made enough, send some to her younger brother. The weekend was however a disappointment. Last night was unproductive. After walking her space for two hours she was picked by a guy who took her to a cheap restaurant and simply wanted to talk when he learnt she was a university student. When he finally called for his bill at 11.20 he had asked her where he would drop her and promised to see her the next day giving her N2k 'for transport.' She had found her way back to her beat but had picked no one for the night. Here she was now with someone who hardly noticed her, not even asked her name.

Anonde maintained a steady speed as he thought over his experienc at Nyanya where he had to park his car along the road and pay for one hour because there was no drive way to the dump site at that time of day. He had to pass through Area B Junction through a stark corridor with the dead end of latrines. He could not think of returning the same path so he made a turn around to his car. He walked towards a man to find out when the road to the dump site would be opened for motorists but the look of this man simply overwhelmed Anonde. He was short, charcoal black and obese but looked strong. He had on a high neck T shirt which stopped just below the last fold of skin below his chin. On his chest was boldly printed New York and below in smaller prints, Bad Boy. His ears pointed right up above his shaved head. His face was round and wide and his mouth occupied most of his face. His nose appeared like a pebble thrown in the middle of a giant cake. His drooping eyes were red and appeared like targeting Anonde who quietly turned and walked fast almost passing his car.

He looked towards the building he had just left wondering which was tolerable, these dead end latrines with the waiting crowd of users or the Dutse bushes and bags flung behind houses which often were another's front yard. Sixty percent of houses in that environment had no toilets, Anonde learnt, and tenants used the nearby bushes some of which were walkways. An escort had led him to a 'dump' which turned out to be a 'big' toilet site. Some people didn't mind being seen doing it and they squatted close to the walkway and did it, looking at passersby who would look away in embarrassment or just look away from the eye of the squatter. When Anonde wondered aloud about the exposure, his escort said some bad people sometimes waited for a lone person in the bush so it was sensible to be close to the road. 'Oga a no blame dem o. Some pupul hide inside de wait for your eye or oda tins for ya bodi. Some go just knak you arand becos of money wey you no get sef.' He was sure it was better toileting near the walkway for safety from thieves and ritualists. When they got to the dump Anonde saw from a distance there was little to salvage.

Anonde looked towards the New York Bad Boy one more time and headed for his car not too far away. As he opened the door to his car, he was surrounded by little Tuareg beggars, their mothers a little distance away begging on behalf of their suckling babies. Anonde looked away from them to the lame and blind across the road beside hawkers who ran across competing with rushing cars, blarring horns and flashing headlights. Some of the hawkers bent close to the drivers or passengers begging them to choose something from an array of sweets, chewing gums, biscuits, popcorn, apples, grapes, handkerchiefs or sunshades. One showed him jewelry in a face towel, 'It is high quality orga and madam will like it. I will give you at half price. It is pure gold.' Another man edged him aside, 'See this wrist watch. It is custom made. The best buy.' Anonde could see these were educated young men. One had told him at a petrol station he graduated 'in Accounting second class upper degree four years ago but cannot get a job. A class mate whose father owned this petrol station and whom I used to help write his assignments and allow him copy his answers during exams gave me this job as a petrol attendant.' He seemed grateful especially during petrol scarcity when he made some good money from tips and black market. Anonde had wondered how good. He did not look like one who earned good money.

He spotted some dustbins which looked empty, with wastes dumped around it. He had managed his way around the milling crowd, long stretch of cars at the traffic lights past rotten cabbages, oranges, vegetables beside the tables of those that sold them. The previous day he had commented on this comfortable attitude of pouring rubbish and sitting with it. People rarely do that in villages so why in the city. His driver had noted that Abuja was for everybody and what belonged to everybody belonged to nobody. Everybody waited for somebody to do something and nobody did it. A few who did soon got tired and learnt to tolerate.

That had been the complaint of a woman in one of the Bonny B apartments in Gwarinpa. She lived on the ground floor and cleaning the compound seemed to be her chore. The rest threw rubbish anywhere but in the rubbish bin which she had bought. She had devised a means of paying the boy who picked from the waste bins in the Close to collect what was thrown around it into the bin. Those on the top floors would eat groundnuts, sugar canes and throw the peels down the front door of the lady on the ground floor and unless you caught them at it, they would deny and abuse you in addition. Once when there was no water, one had thrown her waste in a water bag and the lady on the ground floor had called the police.

Anonde made frantic effort to avoid a pothole in the well laid out road and Attah pitched forward. He pulled her back with an apology. He still had to get used to the city. The light in front of him just before the pothole glowed green and he changed gear and moved on. The hole reminded him of the Bonny B apartments in Gwarinpa on a close on 111 Road where the flood had taken down a fence and washed down a car to the road. The debris that came with the flood also filled the road, much of it around the car its owner and friends were trying to pull away. He had stopped and joined a group of people who stood by and complained bitterly that the fenced off place on a drainage system was an illegal plot sold by FHA to a police commissioner. He said he lived in one of the blocks to which the space sold to the man belonged. A tall slim man in tight knickers asked why they did not complain to the right authorities and reminded them of El-Rufai who would have sent a team down to 'remove that stuff fia! No waste of time.'

Another man who lived in the close said they had written to the F.C.T ministry but nobody had responded to the complaint. 'Any way El-Rufai was no longer there and it is again powers from above.' More cars stopped and very soon AIT news was there and they picked on a woman who had come out in a night dress with her coat on her arm. 'Madam, what is the cause of the flood in your area?' The reporter asked. 'Well this is largely a self created problem by people who are so greedy they have no respect for the city not to talk of their neighbours. Look at that house? I understand it's the owner who has bought the space belonging to these apartments. As far as they are concerned, the occupiers here don't deserve their space. He has fenced in not just their BQ space but the drainage as well.'

'Very true,' said a standby. Others nodded in agreement to what the woman said while others complained and gabbed.

As the gaggled complained loudly and spat and hissed, Anonde found an outlet and drove to the Gwarinpa village to inspect a dump site which turned out to be a collection point which had filled up half the dirt road and the front of two houses. As he moved off, a young man ran into the road closely pursued by a group of men. The young man jumped a ditch but slipped and fell on his face in the debris washed down from the mountain of refuse. Two men caught up with him and dragged him to his feet.

'Where is the money?' One of them asked sticking a finger on his forehead

'Which money?' the thief asked, his narrow red eyes darting from one to another of his pursuers. One gave him a tight fitted blow on the jaw. He staggered back but was held by several hands and as if that blow was a call to action, the mob descended on the young pick pocket mercilessly with stones, broken pieces of wood, belts and blows. Within seconds the man was in a stream of blood running down his nose and mouth and his exposed arms which he used to shield his face.

Anonde drove away sadly being in no position to help the young man. These thoughts reduced his pleasure of the party he had just attended. It was organized by his company to formally welcome him to Abuja. He was adjusting and would get his family to join him soon. He had been promised a job for his wife and he was sure she would love it. As for schools for the children he would wait until she came next week to make a choice of the two schools he had identified by a friend's advice.

'I will stop here,' the girl said suddenly. He slowed down and noticed an area densely populated with people milling around. He slowed down and made to park behind a green bus so the girl could disembark when the girl began to shout. He was startled by the sharp scream from the girl.

'You must pay me my money!' she flung the door open without getting out.

'What money?' the perplexed man asked. The girl grabbed his shirt with fury,

'Pay me my money!' The man glanced at the men who were now coming close. He wondered how quickly a crowd could gather when it was not needed. If it were a robbery, no one would be near until it was done. He looked at the girl who suddenly lost her innocence. Her lips were pulled back from her face, her nose flared and twitched and her eyes bore into him, daring him.

'Wetin?' a woman asked bending down to look at Anonde

'Tell him to pay me my money,' the girl screamed. Two men moved forward smiling, pushing the woman aside. 'It is only two o'clock. Not too long. Man settle the chookoochookoo make she go get another till day break,' said one.

'O ya, make you pay am now! Abi you think na free?' said the second. More people joined the group surrounding his car.

Anonde noticed more people were crossing from the other side of the road towards him. He looked at the girl. It slowly dawned on him that his passenger was a street girl, another scrap. The news would ruin him, and with speed of lightning, he pulled out his wallet and counted five one thousand naira notes and thrust it at the girl. A standerby laughed and muttered loudly, 'Yes throw am for de dust bin breast and go home to ya wife.'

'Foolish man,' Attah said, carefully stuffing the money in her bag with one hand while straightening her blouse, pushing in her breasts which had come loose as she pulled at him. By the time she slammed the door close, the crowd had dispersed as quickly as it had gathered. Anonde heaved a sigh of relief and drove off. This was scrap you avoided, he thought, winding up the screen shield the girl had pulled down

THE UNENDING CLOUDS

Elmina shot hateful looks at her teenage sister Clementina who sat in the garden in the plastic chair the caretaker had motioned her to. She looked past Elmina to the couple taking a walk a short distance away but could see the daggers in her sister's eyes. She was scared, as she had always been with an expression that said, 'I am the only one that cares for you,' which made Elmina more angry.

'Why did you bring me to Shenley hospital? Can't you see this is a mental hospital? Am I sick?' Clementina said nothing, knowing her sister was not done yet.

'Are you crazy? You come to London and the next day I am in the hospital and you are at home with my husband! What are you up to Clementina?'

'The police arrested us and brought us here, don't you remember? Then I went to bed and came back this morning. You were asleep when I left. If you have Kevin's number, I will call him so he can come here as soon as he returns.'

'Tell them to let us go home. I am not sick. Why am I in the hospital? Why did the police arrest me?'

'You drove against the traffic yesterday when we left British Home Stores.'

'So why did they not take me to court instead of bringing me here. I am not sick. You tell them that!' she shouted at Clementina and began to weep as she saw the male nurse approach.

Clementina looked sadly at her sister as the nurse escorted her back into the ward. They would sedate her again and she would be asked to go home till the next day. She followed them, Elmina crying loudly and begging her sister to take her home. She had tried aggression in the morning and she did not want the experience of that restricting jacket anymore.

She had promised to behave and had hoped that when Clementina came as they promised she would they would go home. But here she was annoyingly cool as usual and doing nothing. Elmina looked around her. Even if she ran, she wouldn't get far.

She wept turning once in a while to flash hateful looks at her sister who walked a little behind her and the nurse that led her to the bed and helped her on to it. Then taking her hand, gently injected a drug into it. Within minutes she was asleep. Clementina sat on a chair next to the bed for a while and flipped through a fashion magazine. When she had herself recollected, she put down the magazine, adjusted her skirt and sadly walked to the gate where she signed out and called a cab.

The driver was familiar with the moods of relatives who visited the hospital. He could tell their temperaments by looking at them and he knew the questions to ask. He saw that the black girl waiting for him was greatly disturbed.

'This your first visit to Shenley?' Clementina shook her head, looking at the road in front of her and deliberately avoiding the driver's face. She did not want to talk, least of all about her sister.

'A relative?' The driver would not be put off.

'My sister.' The driver looked at her and she said,'My second visit. Was here yesterday.'

'She will be alright. They all get fine. And you will get used to it. I mean her new behavior. And it won`t be for long. This is a good hospital. Is it drugs?'

'No.'

'Well, that`s a little bit more difficult but she will get over it. And you don`t look that way. How old are you?'

'Sixteen.'

'High school?'

'Just finished.'

'What are your plans? A job?'

'College.'

'Great plans. And today is Friday. Go have fun with your friends. Don`t come back here tomorrow. They have some interesting things for those who are up to it on Saturdays in the hospital. You live your life. Go to a gig tonight. Cheerio,' he concluded as he stopped at the coaches' park for London.

Clementina settled in her seat on the coach and pulled from her bag a copy of the *Tale of Two Cities*. She had been to a book auction in Wembley the previous Saturday with Kevin and had decided to pick all copies of Dickens's books she did not have but had read. Dickens made London a familiar place even to first time visitors. He made you feel on arrival that you knew the city, that you were a part of it. When she walked down some streets window shopping, she could even imagine the wedding dress and old cake of Miss Havisham. But right now she could not concentrate on the book on her legs as she looked down the quiet streets and identical one storey houses with small grassy windows and flowered patches in front of their doors facing the streets. They were so different from the wide open spaces of compounds back home in Nigeria where children played, where few people thought of flowers and where the few sidewalks were taken up by traders in the busy areas.

Clementina adjusted the seat and made herself more comfortable. She had a few friends in London. Sadiq was in Marble Arch and Helen in St. Johns Wood. They had planned to spend the weekend in Dublin. But now Elmina had relapsed into schizophrenia; Kevin was yet to return and she hated to explain the situation to her friends.

Clementina was thirteen when the first signs came one morning at breakfast. Elmina had just married Kevin, a Scots man and Clementina had moved in with her spending her holidays from the boarding school in the large farm house on the farm Kevin, the agricultural economist managed. Clementina had joined the two at a breakfast of bacon which she liked with toasted bread and sausages which Kevin liked with boiled potatoes, and scrambled eggs which Elmina liked with chips. However once in a while they selected the other's favorite for a change. The cook served the choices near each person's seat. Kevin sat opposite Clementina and Elmina at the head of the table and often insisted on serving things on Clementina's plate to her right and Kevin's to her left. She would tell them to have a healthy meal reminding them breakfast was the most important meal of the day. Often Kevin would eat what she placed on his plate and mutter, `nice,' or `naw,' and push it away.

Six weeks earlier when Clementina had come home on a midterm break, she had noticed Kevin rather anxious and jittery. She had asked him what the problem was and he had told her he was trying to quit smoking so Elmina would also stop smoking. Clementina thought that was a wise thing to do, stop smoking first, then encourage those around him. She knew Elmina was very stubborn and a difficult person to convince when she had made up her mind. Perhaps they wanted to start a family, have a baby. Clementina had wondered how they would be smoking in their baby's face when they eventually decided to have one. Her mother had told Elmina when she learnt of their plans to get married to quit.

`And are you going to continue smoking now you want to get married?'

`He smokes,' she had said and left the room.

After the wedding, mother had again asked,`Are you pregnant?'

`No,' Elmina had answered looking at her mother as if she had said something sacrilegious.

`Well, when you plan to, you must stop immediately if you want a healthy child.'

She had nodded and left, lighting a Benson and Hedges Cigar as she got into the waiting car. Perhaps they were thinking of having a child now, Clementina concluded. When Kevin told her he was trying to stop smoking and noticed his shaky hands, she said, `I think you should eat a lot of fruits and drink lemon grass. That's what my friend Georgina's father did when he stopped smoking. He said it helped. He also said he needed to keep on to something so he slaughtered chickens, skinned them or burnt the feather's on open fires, just anything to take his mind off. He said it's terrible when you sat down watching TV or reading a book.'

'Thanks,' he had said, wondering if he could slaughter a chicken. He had seen chickens being cut all the time but he didn't think he could bring himself to it.

'And he jogged in the mornings and walked in the evenings after dinner without money in his pocket so he wouldn't have to stop at a kiosk to buy a stick,' Clementina added.

When she came home six weeks later, at breakfast that morning, as she walked to the table, she saw that awful expression on Elmina's face, staring at Clementina's plate of two sausages and bacon with two slices of toasted bread beside.

'Don't sit there,' she said in a low voice. Kevin looked at her. Clementina stopped just behind the chair looking down at the plate.

'What?' she asked. It was the same thing she had eaten yesterday and many other days. But Elmina was seeing the sausages moving, trying to be something else, a reptile. And she quickly picked the serving spoon from the bowl of oats and slammed at the content of Clementina's plate and Clementina stepped back, one of the sausages at her feet.

'What's it?' Kevin was still holding her. Gradually she sat down and held her head in her hands.

'Sit down and eat your breakfast,' Kevin said to Clementina who picked the sausage on the floor and put it on a side plate, pulled the chair and sat down.

'It's the stress that goes with the attempt to lay off. Your sister is fighting the battle of her life- to stop smoking. Your prescriptions don't seem to work for her as it did with me and your friend's father.' Clementina smiled and sat down but decided not to have anything to do with the sausages. She was relieved. She had been afraid. She could not understand what Elmina saw which they could not. Perhaps it was a witch making an attempt to visit during the day. Witches must be getting very bold now, moving around in the day time.

Kevin took Elmina to their room and Clementina cleared the table. She was looking at an old newspaper when Kevin left for work. She hoped Elmina would soon get over this non-smoking thing and go back to her life which was fast and exciting. A very creative person, she changed jobs like her hats. Since after the college of education eight years earlier, she had just left her fifth job and was doing upholstery until recently when she almost went into seclusion shortly after she started trying to lay off her cigars. Her employers were not just creative or innovative enough to see the rejuvenations Elmina brought into their companies or establishments. At Bata she had suggested that rather than sending a sales person every few minutes to the store to check if the customer's size was available, all available sizes were to be displayed and customers would try the shoes and pick a suitable size. She noted that some buyers were a half size and may decide to go for less or bigger size if they really wanted the design.

The first two days went and the sales girls and boys made less trips to and from the store. However, on the third day a pair of shoes went missing and on the fourth and fifth day, the sales girls were asked to pay for the missing shoes. Elmina said they could display one leg if the security could not keep an eye on the customers. In fact she thought the security shared the greater blame but said she was not paying for the shoes. When the manager suggested that the different shoes were one size and Elmina was one of the two sales girls who wore that size, Elmina was enraged. She slapped the sales manager and quit. Two days later she got a job at singer where she was now assistant sales manager to the highest selling sewing machine manufacturer's distributor in the country.

But she didn't stay long. Clementina heard her telling mother one day when mother asked her about her job that it was the most boring job in the world. She found her position less challenging than that of a sales girl. And the job of an assistant gave you no choice to be innovative. And worse of all her manager presented Elmina's ideas at meetings without acknowledging her. Then one day she gave Madam Manager an inconclusive idea on Xmas bonanza in a raffle draw which would promote sales. Madam Manager was so excited she rushed to the General Manager who asked for an explanation. She took permission to go to the toilet claiming she had eaten something disagreeable. Then she ran to Elmina who refused to give explanations to anyone but the MD himself. She wanted to explain it directly to the MD. The manager was furious and threatened her with a poor recommendation. She said Elmina was an assistant and Elmina's ideas were hers until she became a manager. Elmina told her to go ahead and do the recommendation and decided to close for the day without permission.

23

It was 10 a.m. when Elmina went to Kingsway stores and met the manager who was attending to Elizabeth Arden who was in Jos Marketing her skin products. Elmina was thrilled. She asked Elizabeth a few questions about her oily face and dry skin and the teenage pimples which had persisted to early twenty. She listened to the tips and when she turned to go, the well dressed manager, Gloria Utomi waved a come here sign to her. They moved to the underwear section.

'Where do you work?'

'Singer.'

'As what?

'Assistant manager.'

'You are young.'

'I have experience and I can think and I can talk my way to anything.'

'I saw that over there,' she said pointing to the corner they had just left.

'I just had a quarrel with my manager. That`s why I am here at this hour.' Gloria Utomi knew the manager of Singer. She was not a brilliant woman and not confident enough to effectively use a sharp girl like this to her advantage.

'Not over a man. You are a pretty girl!' She wanted to thaw down the mood. Elmina did mot laugh but was certainly relaxed.

'No. I wanted to give the company a good marketing strategy for the coming Christmas. She would not acknowledge it as my idea.'

'My assistant is on maternity leave and due for a course after. Will you be interested in the position? Kingsway would prefer someone older but you seem to have the experience as earlier noted. I will strongly recommend you.'

'What happens when the other woman on leave and training returns?'

'If you are as smart as I think, she gets another position in another department. This is a multi-product company, not single like Singer.'

'When do I start?'

'Today? What is the name?'

'Tomorrow? Elmina Bur.'

'Good. You will pick your letter on resumption.'

It was an interview concluded and Gloria Utomi was satisfied with the young woman. She was especially impressed when she had told Elizabeth to try Shea butter in her hand cream if she had started producing any hand cream. The young woman was familiar with good local skin products in spite of the fact that most girls of her age were crazy about foreign products and wouldn't touch the local ones. And she was good looking with a fine skin and that crop of hair and lots of confidence. Yes, she could do with a girl like that.

Elmina had gone back to her office to say goodbye to two people she particularly cared about in that work place.

"Ah there you are! The manager's been looking frantically for you!'

'I know. Where is she?'

'In the store. I will call her,' the sales girl said running off.

She walked over to Mr. Udem, the store keeper. He was like a father. You could talk to him almost on anything. Elmina had confided in him and he was a great confidant.

'Good afternoon Sir,' she said checking her time, it was not yet twelve but it would in a short while.

'Good afternoon Elmina. You went out? The manager was looking for you and she looked desperate!'

'She ought to be. I came back only because I want to tell you I am leaving Singer today for Kingsway tomorrow. I just had an interview with them and will give them an idea Singer manager didn't want.'

'Oh I see. But she wants it now and I think that is why she is looking for you.'

'Too late.' Just then the manager came into view.

Mr. Udem moved away as she approached them.

'Elmina, MD wants to see you about our discussion this morning.'

'I am sorry m'am. I am leaving you today. I already have a job and I got the job because of the idea you didn't want or wanted without acknowledging. Please tell MD I can't see him except to say goodbye if you don't mind.'

It was at UTC she had met Kevin while working in the furniture department where she had learnt something about upholstery and decided she would go solo. Then she had agreed with Kevin that now working at home, she would start a family. She knew Kevin loved children and wanted to have his own. It was with this decision that the war to stop the cigarettes started and then this incidence with the sausages.

Clementina was still looking at the newspaper which Kevin had put aside for her, when her friend Polly came in. she didn't hear the car drive in. Polly's father was a head driver at the ministry of Health. They had finished at the same primary school where Polly was always top of the class.

Now in the secondary school she was always tops. The first position was permanently hers and if anyone struggled hard enough, they bracketed. She was three years older than Clementina but it didn`t show much. Clementina was taller and bigger bodied and they liked each other, especially when Clementina gave her a Dunlop mattress in place of the grassy one most girls used in the hostel. Some renovation was done in the farm house and Clementina had asked for the mattress in the guest room which was a little bigger than the one in her her school.

She had taken it to school and given her smaller one to Polly. Polly had sent her own mattress back home and told her father that Clementina had given her a mattress. He had come to look at it and began to appreciate their friendship and since then he would drop Polly himself at the farm house to spend a few days and pick her again.

When Polly entered the the sitting room she found Clementina flipping through the papers. Clementina did not look up thinking Kevin had forgotten something and returned for it. Polly stood by the door, her small bag containing two dresses and pajamas and watched Clementina who suddenly exclaimed,

`Ah now I know why you said I should go through this paper!' She looked up and was pleasantly surprised to see her friend and said,

'Ah so it's you. I thought it was my brother in-law. Come and see our school took first position at the March past and the camera got me real good! Ah but our uniform is great. See the Bolero. And hat!' Polly ran over to see the news item.

They were bent over the paper when they heard Elmina`s cool voice, too cool and hard.

'Come let's go and get something,' she said to the girls.

They both turned towards the voice. She was dressed in pencil pants, a turtle neck blouse and a pair of flat shoes. Clementina looked at the shoes. It was very unlike her sister to wear flat shoes on pants and 'go to buy something.' She headed for the back door where her Beatle was packed. The two girls reluctantly followed, Clementina pulled forward the seat and Polly got in on the back seat.

'Where are we going?' Clementina asked her, settling in the passenger seat beside her sister.

Elmina did not answer her. She started the car and drove out, her eyes focused with such concentration Clementina was scared. She turned to look at her friend who seemed even more frightened. Elmina drove fast to the town where Clementina hoped she was going into a shop to 'get something' and she would call Kevin on a pay phone. But she did not stop. She drove past the town and soon out of town heading towards Kaduna. She had schooled in Kaduna and had worked for a year there.

Why were they going to Kaduna?

'Where are we going?' she looked again at the intensity of her eyes. Elmina smiled mirthlessly and continued driving. Then it dawned on Clementina that her sister did not carry a hand bag! She quickly looked at the fuel gauge. The tank was on reserve! They were six kilometers to Saminaka when the car began to jerk and slow down till it stopped. She tried starting the car. It would not start.

After several trials she asked the girls to come down and push. They pushed the car from the middle of the road to the side. She came down and began to wave down oncoming cars. After the fourth car, a peogeaut 404 stopped.

'Any problem?' the man in the driving seat asked.

'We are going to Kaduna. The car has a problem.' Elmina said sweetly.

'Hop in then.' She was the first to get into the car. Polly remained standing. Clementina walked over to her,

'Let me lock the car.'

'Hurry up then,' she almost shouted.

Clementina walked back to the car and Polly. 'You must go back. This is the number. Call Kevin. I can't leave her. I suspect we may be going to Queen Amina. Tell him I will leave a message there with Mwuese if we are not there when he arrives.'

It was 8pm when Kevin found them. He took Elmina to a hotel not far away. Clementina stayed the night and the next two days with Mwuese. Mother joined them the next day and they moved to a place near the hospital where Kevin had taken Elmina. When mother came Kevin returned to Jos and four days later he was back with two suitcases, one for him and one for Elmina. She was four months pregnant. And they had to leave. A driver took them to Kano and mother and Clementina returned to Jos. Clementina spent a night and a day packing her sister's stuff. She had a lot of clothes and shoes and jewelry. When the cases were all done, Clementina used cartons.

Then the driver took mother and Elmina's boxes and cartons home to Adikpo in a Land Rover followed by the beetle. At 4pm they got to Adikpo and made a left turn from the main road and in less than a minute were in the compound which seemed unusually quiet. The two drivers got down and began to unload Elmina's stuff and move them into the sitting room where mother had shown them.

They refused the food since they had eaten in Gboko barely an hour earlier. The one who had driven the Beetle went back to the car and parked it under the mango tree in the yard. The driver handed the key to mother and got into the Land Rover and in a minute they were gone. The car looked lonely there under the mango tree, and so were the boxes on the floor of mother's sitting room. The owners never returned.

When the boy Kevin junior was born Clementina came to London to stay for a while with Elmina. She no longer smoked. She dressed modestly and talked less. Her nails were kept trimmed and she wore her hair short without a wig. But she still loved to shop even though she had to live on a moderate budget. She now worked at a nearby petrol station. Clementina didn't know what she did there. When Clementina went there Elmina saw her first and came out of a glass walled room where she was seated at a table. Clementina wanted to ask her what she did there but held herself. She could not imagine her sister a few years earlier at home, working in a place like this. She also seemed less aggressive, kind of keyed down. The way white folks looked at one here could key one down. You asked for Marlet Street and they repeated it again to tell you it was not pronounced right the first time. Later Elmina told her how in two different places, a child had touched her skin and ran back to the mother and both had looked at the finger to see if the colour had rubbed off. This happened when they were out of London, in smaller places where people had not seen blacks or not found themselves at close quarters.

Now Elmina had time for Clementina. They talked but she never seemed to say anything that would make

Clementina ask her the question she most wanted to ask her, if she`d like to go home. She was married, had a son and Kevin had left his job at home for her. Clementina didn`t expect her to just leave, but at the same time it did not seem right. The Elmina she saw here was a shadow of the sister she had known all her life.

Now here she was in a coach and her sister in a hospital crying helplessly and she could do nothing. She felt the warmth on her cheeks and lifted her hand to wipe away the tears. She was glad no one chose to sit next to her. She had looked out the window at the few people in the streets- the small houses and the greens and had rarely looked around her in the coach. She now looked around guiltily sure that if anyone of them sat next to her, s/he would have noticed she didn`t turn a single page of the book on her legs and the tears that now rolled down. She suddenly realized how lonely Elmina must have felt in this place away from where there was so much life, where you chose who to visit and who should visit you, where neighbours stopped to say 'how do you do,' and 'how is the family,' and 'it's my birthday, could you stop by at 7pm?' And `my daughter`s traditional marriage is next week and I will appreciate if you will come,' or 'we are opening our new house please join us,' or ` I am washing my new car, its red wine only,' and no matter the dark clouds, the sun would shine. The day before she left for London her friend`s sister dedicated their first boy at a church she could not remember the name, and they danced all evening. Tomorrow Saturday, back home, her cousin Vera will Christen her daughter and it will be dancing all evening and she would miss the fun.

In Nigeria Elmina loved dancing. She dragged Kevin to dances every weekend. Often he enjoyed it but most times he was obviously not at home with the miliki. But he was never lonely, even though often, he was the only caucasian. No one spited him. Clementina now wndered if they went dancing in London as they had danced almost every weekend back home. Elmina who stood up to anyone at anytime back home then had changed. In London now, she was so humble and had cried to Clementina, 'take me home,' 'talk to them.' But she saw that her sister could not help her, the sun refused to shine. Clementina looked up at the unending clouds and sighed. Getting up, she walked up the Isle, out of the coach and headed for Stone Bridge Park.

THE STRIKE

IT WAS EXASPERATING AT FIRST but listening to these conversations about our democracy gave me hope. I had given up on anything ever working for the poor of the country until by conviction I went to the primary school near my house to register for the 2011 elections. I made friends there following the days of struggles to register! These were conversations from acquaintances made within the period and years after. These gaps meant everything to the conversationalists and to listeners including myself at different situations including homes, offices, petrol stations, airport departure launges.

'Ah welcome Izevdonmi. I hope you stocked enough food for the strike. How is the town? I have not gone out today. I was just about to go up the road for papers but okoroafo my neighbor has gone to do that so I am waiting for him. Sit down.'

'Good morning Mvendaga. I did not stock any food. This strike will not last. I drove over twelve kilometers to this place. Everywhere is quiet.'

'Now why do you think the strike will not last. Ah here is Okoroafo with Demola. Sit down gentlemen. I was asking Izevdonmi if he had stocked food. I hope you have, Demola.'

'Sure I have. This is going to be the mother of all strikes. We cannot continue to live with this deceit, poverty and the accompanying insecurity. This party cannot continue to take the people for granted, insult and impoverish them for casting their vote for the man!'

'Now Okoroafo you look pigued'.

'I am not a pig, and don't laugh! This government has absolute respect for the people who voted overwhelmingly for it. You cannot expect the government to sit back and watch a few people reaping the whole nation to, to nothing. I have stocked my house though I believe it will be wrong for labour to continue with this strike. They should give the president a chance to deliver what he is promising.'

'What is he promising? We are sitting out here because there is no electricity since yesterday. My wife just told me she was at the vegetable market a while ago and the Katsina man there told her there is no vegetable for N50 anymore. Look at those boys in front of your house Okoroafor, they live on washing cars. Today not a single person has given them a car to wash because everyone is home and that means no food for them. They live on what they make by the day. Izevdonmi here says the president is no worse than others so....'

'Don't misquote me. I said they just wanted power and would smash anyone who was a stumbling block and the colonial master that created that system supported them.'

'So the country must tow that line. So we must not have a leader that will chart the right course. So we must have people who just come and sit on the power stone, enrich themselves and their families leaving behind more poverty and under development. There is a twenty seven year old girl who served the National Youth Service two years ago. Her father is a senator. She is a director in a ministry. When there is some money budgeted to such a ministry, this inexperienced director goes to consultants who are in turn her father's friends. That's what we go out to vote for?'

'All I am saying is he needs over two years to begin any meaningful changes and he does not need to be a soldier.'

'As I was saying, I bought enough food to last my family three weeks if the strike continues but I think labour should call off the strike and give the president a chance. He is doing well. The people voted for him and we support him. Oil is the only thing we have in this country and those trying to destabilize this country should know that without that oil this country is nothing. For us to move this nation forward we must make sacrifices like we did in the GSM prices. Remember somebody had said telephones were not for the poor but, with GSM lines, the akara seller is now talking on a handset as she turns her akara in the pan. Even those car wash boys you talk about all have their handsets. My wife calls the chicken seller on Saturday morning to get her cockerels ready before she leaves home. And I don't agree with Izevdonmi that Mr. President should sit for two years with 'president' as agenda. He has already set the targets and the subsidy removal is an initiated action towards national development….'

'Now you will tell me, Mvendega, as a minority you must support anyone from the minority groups.' So the whole idea now is minorities don't need to be efficient to counter....'

'For God's sake! This country is not only for the three so called majorities as they are trying to make believe. I don't even believe the president is out to compromise the system. I mean this is a critical time for any leader. This present situation was not created by this gentleman.'

'Well many countries were colonized but have not remained in the shadows of their colonizers. We must move away from that irritating constant resort to the past for everything we fail to do right. You must explain to me what you mean by his not having to be a good man or a tough man. Whatever he is or is not is of no interest to me and lots of Nigerians like me. What is of interest is whether we can drive to other parts of this country without fear of bad roads, whether the farmer can easily move his product and cash without fear of getting robbed, whether the barber will go to work and make some money without spending it on generating his own electricity. We talk of powerful leaders around the world like America and China et al. It is not muscle power because I have not seen them in the boxing or wrestling ring. Why must we focus on divisions and fear of our leaders' powers if such constitutional power is converted into a powerful country. Our personal fears must not become national fears and we must not stand on divisions to fight ourselves.' He turned to Demola who cut in,

'I was saying I can't stand people playing down serious issues for personality issues. Hundreds of people are killed every day in very suspicious circumstances and Izevdonmi says it is being over played. The Niger Delta militants were not overplayed, the Libyan guns coming into Nigeria is not overplayed, the popular booming helicopter business for politicians and preachers to safely move around is not overplayed. The dollar now being used as legal tender making the naira valueless is not overplayed. When I talk about it, it becomes overplayed …..'

'You may say why is Mvendaga against this whole talk of minority when his people have been the most oppressed of minority groups in this country. Okoroafor would not have voted for me if I contested elections as a minority. Izevdonmi would have in fact counted me among the northern group. But I tell you my interest is in how the ordinary people fare in this country because 98 percent of people are ordinary people and will vote again for Awolowo or Abiola who had an agenda for minorities as well as majority. Azikiwe fought for independence and freedom of the oppressed all over the African continent. He was a Pan-Africanist. Zik wanted Nigeria to be a leading nation, not an Igbo majority power lording it over others. He wanted things done right, not this maiming and killing and bombing of churches, police headquarters and government institutions with a police force that implicates itself. Demola would not have voted for them, so stop irritating my ears with this minority thing.'

'Something different, in what way does it change our lives…'

'Whether you agree or not, whether you believe I voted because of oil and personal gain, I still believe there is hope for Nigeria. And I don't agree with Izevdonmi that the president is sitting for over two years to find the door. He is making efforts to increase refining capacity; see what the minister….'Okoroafor wringed his hands trying hard not to shout.

'For God's sake! Minister says what? That new refineries will be built in the near future? Was a refinery not abandoned because a cobra made a home there to hatch its eggs some years back? That there is a team searching for contractors in Japan in shopping malls? Where is the report of the Green field refineries to be sited in Lokoja and some other places which was to be submitted in September? This is January! Where are the "package of palliatives cum incentives to mitigate the impact of subsidy" as was quoted by this minister? Okoroafor will take us back to 1960 when we were going to have water, electricity, roads and schools. We know it was only the western region that fulfilled to some extent its promises. What of the East? Your boys are busy supporting oil and have left education to the girls. Good, let the girls go to school and perhaps they will fulfill better those promises. The North? Izevdonmi may give us a clue to why it's promises are still unfulfilled….'

'Well history can tell you that. The colonialists created a north with a deliberate policy to keep it backwardly educated and the autocratic traditionalists who were afraid of losing control must attack the north's educational backwardness and poverty,' said Izevdonmi.

'As I said earlier, Tiv Division was marginalized by the colonial, the northern region and finally the independent federal government. Education is higher in Tivland than most parts of this country yet we are marginalized. Go to the remotest Tiv village and every man and woman under fifty you meet has been to school and it is evident in the

English they speak irrespective of mixing r and l. You will not see that in Ondo or Ekiti or Oyo states. And they are not fighting to catch up with anyone because they have the man power but we do not aim at any time to destroy the advantages of others. We work hard any where we find ourselves yet we are marginalized!'

'Yes someone needs to answer that question. And I insist it is not by sleeping that you tackle serious issues someone may see as being overplayed. Check out your riots of 1960-1966. Have the issues been properly addressed. If labour has any sense, this strike must go on until the issues are addressed. A managing director said the other day that but for concessions, Nigeria's port system would have collapsed. How can a country like ours have no Nigerian marine pilots but Pakistani's and Indians? If you ask now someone will tell you, we are training them but where are the ships? Now here comes a pleasant change. Mrs. Mvendaga, good morning'.

'Good morning all. James serves the tea while I pass round the cookies and garden eggs. I can see you are all having a break from your offices though I wonder if you deserve this break again after the long Christmas break from which many did not and have not returned. Okoroafor how is the family? I have not seen your wife in a while.'

'Thank you for this lemon grass tea. It is good and from your backyard. You should try the cassava bread the president presented. It is wonderful and affordable. My wife is doing fine. After a recent conference organized by the Society of Engineers, she has decided to leave the university and join the society's research and development unit.'

'O that's wonderful although the universities need good teachers like her. Mr. Demola, I learnt you travelled.'

'Yes, to attend a conference of Heads of Government of the commonwealth. I had to answer some questions on the nation's mining and minerals industry. It was not a very pleasant experience when you must speak well of things that are not well in your country and people around you know the situation too well. Okoroafor's wife is leaving the university with its poor infrastructure where teaching and learning is complicated by an agency which spends billions on training abroad, money that can be used to upgrade facilities and teaching at local universities and draw in the foreign teachers. ASUU is on strike asking the government to equip local universities, but for political reasons it is easier to open new universities without electricity. Look at the Federal Capital University which should be a model of what Nigerian educational system is. Well it is a real model of where no one wants to be. The teachers are all leaving for private universities. The new staff are scavengers called contract teachers who come to the city for different reasons other than teaching.'

'Ah now don't grudge Mrs. Okoroafor. I am also leaving the university but into a private business. I love teaching and I am sure Mrs. Okoroafor does but how do you work in a most uncondusive atmosphere. You have been to my office. We had to talk outside under the tree. We could not even receive phone calls. I remember you were bitter because you wanted to get your niece; you needed to get me the course of her choice for admission. We could not stay in the office because of the heat in the poorly ventilated room. Sometimes I buy paper to get exams done. Sometimes I go to the business center to photocopy exam question papers because the photocopiers have broken down and it could take months to get a response to our request for a replacement. And often normal academic requests including promotions are turned down because you are not 'a friend'. I teach fifteen hours a week and there is no earned allowance. Half my students receive lectures by rumour. They are outside and will ask the person by the window who asks the person inside what the lecturer just said that others are clapping! A head of department gets ten thousand naira imprest to run the office with hundreds of students. And market women are asked to march on the streets asking ASUU to go back to class. I guess this is the same in the ministries and government agencies. Did I not hear people who go to report cases at police stations pay for the paper and biro they write their reports? The only places where quality of staff matters are private businesses. They pay well but people prefer the government where they go for christmas a week before and two weeks after, where if you have someone from 'above' you don't even need to go to work especially if you are from the 'majority' Izevdonmi has been talking about. I think Mvendaga should know what it means being a minority. He is often called upon to clean the mess some majority has made and quickly moved when it begins to pay off. He needs to move too.'

'I am moving nowhere. I don't mind the clean up if someone comes along, recognises it and equips it for the general good. And like Okoroafor, I believe there is hope for our country. Don't forget the failed state prediction of 2015 which has shifted now to 2030. Don't let them actualize it and we won't achieve that prediction if we focus on Nigeria rather than region, ethnicity, majority and minority. We can achieve it through justice and fair play. When every governor begins to identify with the people like Lagos is doing, when politicians stop seeing the states as their bank accounts from where they buy houses in Dubai and UK and set up private universities in Nigeria and neighbouring countries, then the predictions will come to naught. It is only then that Nigerians will be a proud people like in the days of Murtala and proudly show patriotism on their t-shirts and in their passports.'

'Mrs. Okoroafor told me she has met Nigerians in the UK who claim to be Liberians.'

Mrs. Mvendaga said with disbelief, 'I am shocked that a Nigerian will rather be a Liberian in a foreign country!" But I have seen many who are Seira Leonians or some other nationals. When your house is in disorder, you are ashamed to show it off. But that's only when you are lazy to clean it. With the right infrastructure, many will not even want to go to foreign countries driving taxes, selling newspapers and sweeping streets.'

'I just heard on radio that government will now pay salaries on the 20th of the month.'

'That is good but it is no news. My son said the other day he never hears what has been done. It is always what is to be done. He is nine. At twenty he will still hear the same things being done by the same person in a different political party. Let me hear 'the tomato bottling/canning factory in Adikpo begins production today or the fruit juice factory in Gboko opens its doors to customers.' Let me hear people say, electricity is steady in Katsina Ala. Let me see people building their small homes because they can afford cement and roofing sheets and fittings. That will be news. What do you say Izevdonmi?'

'Give the gentleman time. It is still too early for these expectations. It took Britain…'

'Britain did not have any technology at its disposal as we have man! All we need to do is copy it and even improve it to suit our weather, environment and cultural life ways. We were at the same spot with the Asians. They are not waiting for the years it took Britain who colonized them…'

'Ah Mrs. Okoroafor, you are welcome. It's good for you to join me and these men here. I was beginning to feel logged out with these guys' tribal sentiments. Congratulations on your new job but I still think the university will lose a lot without you.'

'Do not bother yourself. Some will be glad. The staff will not care because a position is created. Many want positions even when they know they can't do the job. All it means is the title and for some the possible situations for a bribe once in a while. For some, it is an opportunity to be mean to colleagues or to give favours to friends or make new friends with the perks of office. The students? Hehehe e! 'That strict Okoroafor. That woman that you give her ordinary Christmas card, 'what is this?' If you go to her house, 'is this office?' Nobody gets an A in her course. What can you write for her to get an A? She will send the students she supervises to other universities for research! You write your project, she knows it's a copy, sometimes even the university from which you lifted the work in spite of the fact that there is no computerized network. Let her go. Na only her be lecturer?' No one will miss me o; so do not bother.'

'Is that what the system has become?'

'There is no system, my dear. Right now people are beginning to refer to Vice chancellors as 'chief executives' and they are living up to it. They tell a head of department 'you are my appointee and if you can't do what I want, right or wrong to my satisfaction, you are free to resign the appointment.'

'I do not believe you.'

'There is a lot you will not believe but it is a mad house. Someone who has left described it as a house of horror he could no longer stomach. Goodmorning Izevdonmi. It has been a while.'

'Well you are now enjoying yourself in the petrol dollar sector and have forgotten your poor brother here. I have heard worse things said about the Boko University, it remains to be renamed Haram. I left teaching many years ago as much as I liked the nobility of the profession. I could see it coming decades ago. The ASUU has totally neglected its own members and constituency. Like most labour leaders it has become where this position will take me. Now they are talking as if asking for reward is an anathema. In some universities, the clerks in the bursary and registry have better furnished and more comfortable offices than senior lecturers. At Boko, senior lecturers share offices. Some heads of department share offices with their secretaries. But this is a common situation in most establishments, particularly institutions, it is the degeneration which set in with the military and needs to be addressed by the democratic process which we must all give a chance to germinate.'

'I see you looking at your time, Demola. You may all stay for lunch.'

'I must leave now. Izevdonmi's talk of chance and time reminds me of gender and equality discourse. There is no end to it. I must leave now. I can see Okoroafor also ready to leave. We will walk together. Enjoy this strike and be a part of history.'

'Ah listen to that. Mvendaga increase the volume of that radio.'

'Labour has announced the suspension of the strike as government reduces the price of oil from ninety percent to sixty percent. All filling stations are advised to readjust their pumps to the specified figures. The police will go round to ensure compliance and any station found in the contrary will be shut down. Civil sevants are advised to return to work immediately.'

'That is fast action, you must agree with me. I am sure the ASUU issue will soon be laid to rest too, it wont be too far.'

In the distance was a loud sound and people were running in no particular direction. The two men stopped and looked at each other. A young man of about twenty-four slowed down and shouted, 'They have bombed the market. Many people don kpai.'

'Which market?'

He pointed behind him and ran off. The police sirens could be heard in the direction the young man was heading. A pickup van sped past with some police men with masks and guns sitting on the benches. Another one passed by the men who looked after the Black Maria, and then at themselves. They turned on their heels and hurried back to Mnvendaga's house. They met the others sitting in the same positions they had left them and took the empty chairs they had recently vacated.

'It is a bomb.'

'We heard it.'

'It's the market.'

'Which one?'

The two men looked at each other. 'I think we will join you for that lunch offer.'

Isa walked to his master and squatted. He looked worried but Mvendaga had been with Isa for eight years. 'Someone has made you angry Isa.'

'Yes sir. One man came to buy our registration voter card. He offered us two thousand, then five, then ten. Some of the boys have sold there own.' Everyone kept a neutral face. The women showed some concern which quickly wore off.

'Have you sold yours?'

'Never.'

'Good. We talk later.' Isa stood up, the worry frowns still on his face. Last week his daughter had a fracture in one rib. He had gone home to Ingawa in Katsina state. Many of the young men were not registered and the few registered ones were selling off their cards. They were jobless and broke and when someone came offering two, five or even ten thousand! They saw it as a great offer for just a card they spent a few hours to get. They were not even aware of the implications. Yet they were at rallies shouting their support. He wondered where the organizers were and when they would create awareness to these people. He walked away sadly.

THE PILOT LIGHT

I LOOKED AT MY FRIEND carefully, trying to see some sign. Her beautiful nose sat in her well formed narrow face, twitching a little. She tightened her full lips every few minutes drawing out her pointed chin like a sulking child. She kept her eyes on a sheet of paper with bold scribbles of a poem:

Festivals?
The participants?
Ijaw and Birom youths?
Oodua or Gbesu?
Ha, all ferreting for ethnic interests I call
State of unequal opportunities
Festivals fester the wounds in our psyches

I couldn't turn the page with my eyes and I returned to her face with a marvel. My friend also wrote poetry which appeared sensitive and committed.

'Well, what are you starring at?' she accused me without taking her eyes off the yellow sheet, tears in her eyes, worry lines etched around them.

I shifted my gaze above her head to the open window from which various flowering plants fanned in pleasant air. The unflinching frangipanis stood there, their leaves solid, unyielding to the gentle wind. The well kept, well cut whispering vines teased me with their umbrella shaped spread, daring me to come closer. The wind blew the corn plants at the far corner by the brick fence where the fat gardener suffering from a cold occasionally blew his nose and wiped his hands on the bricks and then on his trouser bottom. That single action took something out of the beautiful scenery.

I returned my gaze to Aje, followed her eyes past the yellow sheet and overstuffed Ottoman to her left and to the beautiful portrait of her mother which hung on the big organ. It was not difficult to see where she inherited her beauty. She had bought that huge musical instrument the previous year and adorned it with expensive silver and gold plated flower jugs and small beautiful picture frames without any pictures. Another yellow sheet on the organ:

Timeless is the creator
Timelessness is the mystery
Not the father-son-spirit
To whom one thousand years is but a day
can father be without spirit?
without sons in whom he invests,
touches and leaves a mark on the world?

I was amused at this shopping spree of items which seemed so out of place. And the stories... poems...the writings.

I followed her eyes to her enticing mahogany corner behind which two glass shelves with choice brandy and wines, crystal glasses and silver beer mugs invited you to partake. Yet Aje never drank anything but Ribena disguised in a neat bottle of Yago. I walked over and helped myself to this bottle, showed her a glass to which she shook her head in impatient refusal. I sat in the cane chair by the entrance, in which she often pointed to people whose company she did not wish to keep long. She suddenly straightened and walked hurriedly to the big chair behind which she lifted a container and spat in.

Watching Aje spit in that sand filled chocolate box brought back apprehensive memories. Rather than pity, I watched her carefully with a spice of suspicion. Was she really pregnant or just faking? Like I had done ten years ago. Oh.... But that was different. I had hated the idea of towing a pregnancy to the altar as my fiancé and his people had expected. Yes. Women, especially the educated had to prove their fertility; the men had to ensure the security of having children to secure their family line. The women must acquiesce for the sake of the ring, the passport to respectability.

So when I hesitated after my engagement, refused getting pregnant before my beloved would fix the date, the cards, the shopping, the gown and the trip to St. Bartholomew's for a white wedding that wouldn't be so white, my beloved showed surprise. 'Did I think I was too young?' He had asked mischievously. Didn't I realize this was my peak in the marriage market,' his amused face seemed to say. I assured him it was not so much the age but the things I believed were necessary for two working people to do before going into the 'limited' horizon of marriage. I did not add that a sensible woman around for a while knew that a man's affection wanes as his wife adds the years and the Kids. And so does his finances. His vision of love is absolutely limited to taut breasts and buttocks. A woman must be prepared for when love and finances wane. At such a time she could always live on her pre and post marriage investments. I also wanted to enjoy his intellect, his humour; to know him, learn to love him- a love that will purify my heart and not the pride love, the body love we had shared this past few years. That love choked me; it killed something vital in me. I wanted to settle down into a job in which my potentials would be fully utilized. And when my first baby came it would be a crown. But thoughts of my skills development sent my love into deeper thoughts which made him withdrawn and sad. Couldn't I see that he loved me and was getting too old waiting for me? We could marry, have children and nothing will change. It was obvious why he chose this night. He knew my woman cycle and he knew this was the time to make a baby. He also knew I was not on the pill because my Catholic mind resisted the pill.

Aje had advised that just this once or this period that I had things on the drawing board I could pop an 'occasional' when it wasn't safe and feign illness when the period was on. That way I could keep him guessing while I did my thing. But my Catholic conscience hardened against this advice. It was easier to confess a lie than a pill. So I took a trip next day to see mother, came back five days later, wore a pad and pretended my red letter day came at a wrong time because of stress. I assured him it was normal. He could start counting again. I watched the worry lines disappear from his handsome face. He nodded and gathered me into the hard comfort of his arms, his taut legs locked around me. Cultural differences were especially hard on women. Perhaps if some of us educated women didn't try so hard to build bridges….. Perhaps stay within your tribe, your clan. Back home it would be a great shame for me to go pregnant to the altar.

'She forced herself on the poor man,' accusing fingers would say.

'He is a gentleman. He had to marry her because of her deceit,' others would explain.

'And he is too sympathetic to admit,' they would say when he tried to tell the truth. Yet here she was going through intrigues because Ade came from a society where a girl had to 'PROOVE because it all depended on her.'

A day before the real thing, unknown to him now, he travelled counting the days when she would be due for motherhood. When he returned the danger was days away. He sowed seeds in infertile soil and waited. A month passed and Ade was sure I was in the family way. Second month he couldn't contain the silence and my cheery disposition. He asked. I laughed and went out and wrote my M.A exams merrily. Three months. I finished work on the first draft of my thesis, applied and got a well paying job with the National Research Institute. Fourth month I considered my beloved's worries. I began to put on healthy kilogrammes of meat and carbohydrate. Fifth month, I started to spit and retch whenever my beloved was in town. He noticed. He was overjoyed. He scribbled a programme and asked me to fix a date for the printer. One morning he brought a bag of money for shopping. I added a few more kilogrammes, happy with my job, with the results of examinations, with the final draft of a work my supervisor thought was a rare piece of literature and advised I found a publisher. Ade and his family and his friends rejoiced at my smooth skin, healthy kilos. I worried only of one thing. Weddings embarrassed me to no end. Friends and neighbours made weddings sound like a circus, like two people masquerading before a group of food hungry, party hungry and marriage hungry people. Most irritating was the suggestive remarks made at such gatherings. I was party shy, crowd scared, especially the wedding crowd which reminded me of some doom, the women in King George. I felt like a Christian on her first visit to a shrine. Yet Ade and I must go through it, shop and prepare for St. Bartholomew, happy that if for nothing else I would have a white wedding.

Two weeks later as Ade and I rolled on the carpeted floor of an Amsterdam hotel room celebrating our wedding away from our crowded rooms of family and friends, I felt the cramps. I knew that tonight junior would be made. The kilos of meat and pounded yam will stop, that of my God given baby will grow. But I wouldn't ruin my honey moon; this beautiful week I was sure would not repeat itself.

Today however I watched Aje as she spat and ate kola. She was thirty two, tall, full-bodied, beautiful. She was branch manager with a well established bank, an interior decorator who romanced with colours and painted beautiful portraits of people and landscape. She had gotten herself pregnant so that Uche her boyfriend of five years would fix a date. But Uche had asked her to see a doctor, to 'remove it.' Aje had asked him who he thought she was, a school girl? There were shouts and accusations of things done 'behind my back' and cries of 'go to hell'. The door had slammed. Here she was spewing and chewing furiously at bits of kola it was obvious she did not enjoy.

'I am not having an abortion. Apart from the action being wrong I want what I am carrying. So Uche is good looking and holds a good job. So do I. But he is not a child and shouldn't let it go to his head that several women put themselves out to be nice to him. I will go through this and I don't care what mama or anyone says. And I will make sure Uche shares or at least recognizes paternity even if we don't get married.' I looked at her with love. She said,

'Ene I'm going to depend so much on you. I know you understand. I don't care so much about the marriage bit you know. I just want my babies from one father and then I can face the world. And when the men stop caring my babies will care. Can you show me one woman who wouldn't give anything for this Pilot Light?' I nodded.

Many things began to fall in place, the car, house, furnishing, new interests. I looked at the potted geranium by the window, the big rubber plant against the wall, the woolly floors. I wondered why she said babies. If Uche didn't come back, how was she expecting the next? Aje was like most women of her generation, ambition, riches and success. They married late – some for dignity of title and most for one main important reason- one woman reason, to have babies, motherhood, and the limit of woman desire- to fulfill God's purpose of creation. Like Eve, to live a thousand years, to look on her children with a secret pride of knowing the humans God had used her to bring to earth; of watching with amusement same historical continuities her sons think are peculiar to them; of seeing her daughter recreate the same feats of giving birth to life.

I turned with a satisfied grin to see Aje looking out through the window with that cunning, secret look in her woman eye. My woman mind identified the basic desire in that eye, a common goal. It reminded me of Amaka who said she was prepared to walk on her head, her legs held up if that was the only way to keep from a feared abortion. Every woman there had laughed knowing each of them would do that if the doctor said that was the only way. But she did not walk on her head. She had chosen to stay in hospital for months so she would not be tempted to walk, cook, lift things. And it had gone well. Her only regrete was 'I should have taken the fertility bit and made two or three at one sitting.'

Aje travelled home to her village in her fourth month to see her mother and give her enough reasons not to visit too soon and to get a stay- in house help. I was to also arrange a day woman, preferably one who was through with nursing her own babies. She planned and sketched swings and sets of garden chairs, squares and circles of carpet grass play pens, flower beds of pink, red and white roses. She arranged for a pickup load of sharp sand and poured it under a frangipani tree. She got a rabbit pen built and started a lettus garden patch.

Aje returned with her house help, a beautiful fourteen year old girl whose young virgin breasts pointed at me like an accusing finger. Aje grew bigger. She continued to work ignoring her colleagues' questioning eyes and driving them like a foreman. She turned her garage into a 'Designer's Outfit', bought sewing machines, catalogues, employed two Ghanaian tailors and one Philipino lady who forced fear and discipline into the staff and customers even though her knowledge of tailoring was restricted to patches and roughly sewn pyjamas. It wasn't long before the place needed expansion. Aje put in two more prefab rooms that included a 'Hair Salon'.

She said, 'This is good security for the babies while I am at work you know. And the house too.'

I looked at the setting and was sure Aje's baby would just be fine. Not like Omo who desperately wanted to live in the palace as a queen and her son a prince. She chased the eldest prince all over town and one night after a dance got him into bed. He went for his condom but she assured him she was on a fibroid treatment that was also pregnancy protective. She pushed the condom away and he gave in. A few months and her relatives were knocking on his door and asking what he wanted to do with Omo's pregnancy. The Prince would not hear of it and asked her to do whatever she wanted with her pregnancy. It was not long before people began to call Omo and the Prince on radio stations asking when the wedding would be. The Prince stood his ground though worried, knowing that if the baby turned out to be a son, he would be taken to the palace whether or not he married her. But Omo was not so lucky. Junior was a girl. She would not go near the palace. I felt sorry each time I saw her and wish she was wiser. But then she had believed she was very wise and had said, 'I don't care if he leaves after the church but we must get married. This is the first grandson of the king.'

Final month. Aje brought in two great cots. I was alarmed. Then she applied for maternity leave and dared anyone to question it. Her maid Agnes and I sat with her in hospital waiting.

'It is painful isn't it?' she asked me.

'Very: it helps to say the rosary. You know the Virgin Mother went through it. She understands. She makes it easier.'

'How long?

'Never the same as the next person. But as I said the Mother of Our Lord made it easier for me. Short labours too. Two to four hours but the real pain only lasted for about ten minutes, just remember your breaths. It helps.'

She took my hand and said: 'It has started.'

'Remember the joyful mystery?'

'Yes.'

'Now.'

I looked around the hospital room, bare except for the bed; two chairs and a small cabinet on which was arranged Aje's basket of beverages, hot water bottle, flasks and cups. The room smelt sweet, very unlike the sterile antiseptic odour of hospital rooms. 'Home Away from Home' the notices proclaimed. They were right, for a price indeed.

Aje squeezed my hand. She was sweating but still managed to remain calm. 'I think it is coming' she said in a forced but calm voice. I ran for the doctor.

I followed them into the labour room. Aje held tightly unto my hand. For the first time she looked small, scared like a little child. I said, 'You are doing fine. You will be okay'.

We helped her unto the table. Her feet were strapped to stirrup-like poles which made her look like she was being crucified. The nurse pulled her down to make room for the warring one. Aje closed her eyes, gripped the edge of the table with one hand and my hand with the other. She took a deep breath at the same time squeezing my hand so hard I moaned but remained there knowing she needed that hand. She held her breath, her face contorted, lips muttering, 'Holy Mother of God'. Her breathing was all wrong.

'Exhale,' I murmured, touching her face with my free hand.

'That's good', the doctor encouraged. 'Do that again, stronger. That's it!'

The baby shot out like a base ball, legs kicking, a finger in her red smeared lips. The doctor handed it to the nurse, pressed Aje's stomach which was still heaving. 'Relax now. It won't be long.'

I looked at the doctor, then Aje's stomach. I was flabbergasted. I looked at her in alarm. She searched for my hand, her eyes closed, teeth clenched. I began the rosary, counting my fingers, starring unseeingly at the fan blades above me. I must have been on the third decade when a violent tug and the doctor's cry of 'There!' forced me to look at the next baby being handed over to a nurse

'It's a boy', she announced.

'Last one to go and it is impatient?' My mouth hung open. I looked at Aje. She returned my look, eyes moist, pleading, asking me to hang in there with her to the end. I brushed hair from her face, gentle, assuring. She was brave and I loved her for it, even more for her determination. I began to ask God to forgive her, if there was anything sinful in her action, to see her to the end of this ordeal. I began to say 'Our Father'. I could read her lips as she said the Hail Mary asking for our Lady's prayers, telling her she, Aje, knew the prayers of the mother of Jesus were portent and that her prayers would open a window of God's mercy even when her own sins had shut her out.

'Now', the doctor called. Aje pushed. Everyone in that room seemed to push, to sweat, to labour with her at Simon's coming. Tears flowed freely mingling with sweat. Yet Aje simply glowed, smiled. 'I was expecting two', she winked at me. 'But I got a bonus. I am glad though that they weren't more'. I looked at my wrist-watch. It was 4.20 pm. I had to go arrange some hot soup for her. She would need it.

I watched as she ate hungrily. 'What will you call the girl?' I asked. 'Mary, Uche and Simon. The last is after my grand-father. He always said I' d go places, that I looked like a girl who'd have all her children at one sitting and go to work the next day. I don't think he ever heard of fertility drugs.'

I looked at Aje and suddenly it all came home. As we roared with laughter, the door opened. It was Uche, his mother and two sisters. I looked at Aje. She was calm and controlled. I could hear the bells. A new generation had again triumphed, God's creation, God's culture.

DREAMS AND STARS

IT DID NOT ALL START on the day the Indian told me of the bright star that illuminated my existence. I had first heard it from my father, my brother in-law, the Egyptian, the cinema owner, the legislator and a few others like this Indian whom I knew I would not see again. The Indian had kept a watch on me the moment I stepped on the London bus. At first I was engrossed in Alice Walker's *The Color Purple* and paid little attention to those around me but each time I looked up as I turned a page I would catch the man calmly starring at me with those large penetrating eyes under bushy brows. After a while it seemed the eyes were piercing holes into my consciousness. I could not go on with my book and I refused to look up but I could feel, no, see his eyes settle on my forehead, waiting for my eyes to look up. He had a good set of teeth and seemed conscious of them because he frequently opened his mouth and raised his tongue, brushing it around the upper and then the lower set. A few times he simply opened his lips like in a smile keeping the teeth clinched and all the while looking at my forehead or nose, waiting for me to look up so he would catch my eyes.

The bus stopped in answer to a bell. Two old women stepped down slowly. I watched their feet and backs. The Indian kept his gaze. The door closed and I looked out the window. The bus moved on and I looked ahead. There was a park in the distance and I put a marker between the pages of my book, dropped it in my bag, stood up, walked to the door and pressed the bell. The bus pulled over and the door slid open. As I stepped down the last step, the Indian was right behind me. I had the intention of sitting in the park to read this wonderful book, now I wasn't so certain. I turned to face the man, 'What do you want?'

'Let us sit. You are a lucky girl with a wonderful star.'

'What about the star?' I asked in a calm voice. I was not afraid. I had never been afraid, not even of the dark when I was a child. And this was a park in St. John's Wood. There were many people around and I didn't believe the man could cast any spell on me. I walked to a bench and he sat next to me and asked me to show my hand. I showed him my palm and he prophesied many great things. I gave him my sweetest smile and let him touch my nose. Then I told him I had to read for a session the next day and we fixed a date. We would have lunch and go to some place where he would show me how to actualize my future, by which time I would have been in Aberystwyth.

I was not afraid of dating. My first date was at 11, with my father. My mother had travelled to Zaria to buy stuff for my sister's traditional marriage. That night, my father sent the boys to bed early. He asked me to finish my homework which I had not had time to do. He had burdened me with household chores which I normally did with my two brothers. Today he had sent them to do their assignments and sent me with a message to Aunty Hembadoo. I was surprised the boys had not washed the dishes and so I had to do the washing up. By the time I was through the boys had finished and it was time for siesta which was often enforced. I had hoped I'd do my work when the others went to play ball but dad again sent me on an errand to uncle Ioriam. Aunty later came and I had to assist her with dinner. We ate, did the dishes, cleaned around and bathed. Aunty had left by the time I sat down to my homework.

When I finished my assignment, the house was quiet. I packed my bag, placed it on the side table and went to my room which I had shared with my sister but now had it all to myself, first when she went to boarding school, then to Makurdi as a sales girl with U.A.C and this weekend she would be married and I would own the room. I had changed into my night dress after my bath before I went to write my homework on the dining table so I just dropped off after a short night prayer.

My breasts had just begun to sprout and they were the size of small lime fruits. They were part of my chest now and they often got exposed when I slept. I was a 'bad sleeper', my sister had said as I often got my dress all shifted to my chest. I often caught colds because my night dress covered my face more than my body. When my sister was here she insisted I wear pyjamas and made it a rule that no one entered our room without knocking and waiting until they were called to come in. Now I had the room and slept in my night dresses which my father bought for me. Everyone knocked before entering my room at night. Tonight I was tired and slept deep because I had no siesta.

My small lime size breast must have been exposed to the cold because they tingled as if something warm was brushing them. At first I thought it was a dream as they tingled and swelled. It felt so good I thought the angel that we asked to keep us company at night was playing with me. Then I felt something wet and warm like when my dog Lucky licked my hand and in my dream I stretched apart my legs and it was so warm and I began to shake with a strange feeling. It got so tense I brought my legs together and there seemed to be a head between them and the sensation was so heavy I grabbed the pillow above my head, my body shook and twisted and then I was totally relaxed and fell asleep. I thought I heard the door open and gently close but I could neither move nor open my eyes. This was a sweet dream, almost real.

When I woke up, I felt a little tight around my 'legs' as mother often called that place. I touched it and bent down to look at it. Everything seemed normal. I pulled down my nightie and rolled out of bed. I lifted my left foot off the floor in fear and disgust. Did I vomit in the night without being conscious of it? I looked at the sole of my left foot, something slimy dripped from it to the floor and there was more of it on the ground. I looked closely, it couldn't be okra? We ate egusi with pounded yam last night. I went out and picked a newspaper and returned to my room. Did I do this? I looked around me. I saw a wall gecko. Did they do this? Is this their shit or piss? I wiped it and took the paper out and threw it in the pit where we put rubbish. As I turned to return, I saw my father standing under the lemon fruit tree. He was looking at me more intently than normal

'Good morning, papa.'

'Morning. Are you ok?

'Yes.'

'You slept fine?'

'Yes, papa'. How could I tell him I had a dream that was strange?

'What is that you are throwing off?'

'I don't know, papa. Do lizards shit/piss?'

'That's not an intelligent question.'

'I am sorry. It looked like blended okra on the floor beside my bed.'

'Maybe from you but don't talk about silly things. You want people to laugh at you?'

'No, papa. Maybe it was the dream.'

'You dreamt! It is common to dream when you are growing up. Just keep it to yourself.'

'Yes, papa.'

The second time I had this dream was shortly after my twelfth birthday. My mother had travelled to Kaduna to be with my sister who had just had a baby. That afternoon I had complained of headache and as we prepared for bed, my father gave me Panadol and an additional medicine. He said it was a vitamin. That night the dream came twice. I could feel the tears role down my ears.

When I woke up there was again that sensation. I touched and looked down but it all seemed just ok but this time there was a dry spot on the bed. It was a dirty white and I was certain this was from me. Did it come from my privates? My mother had said I should start my menses any time. Perhaps these were the symptoms. I should ask mother when she returned. But I didn't and everything seemed just fine.

Four days after mother travelled, papa bought those vitamins again, two this time. I wondered why he didn't give the boys. Perhaps girls needed more vitamins. I was heavy with sleep but I could feel the pains. I felt the pains vibrate all around my 'leg'. I opened my mouth to scream but a hand was firmly there. I could not open my eyes but I could smell, and it was my father's smell. I held my lips tight. I could feel the gentle heaving and then some sounds. I lay there unable to move, unable to open my eyes and then I felt a wet towel cleaning me out and I fell asleep.

I woke up in mama's bed with pains in my 'leg'. The house was silent. I got up and could barely walk to the door. When I pushed it open a chair that had been leaned against it fell. Papa came immediately.

'You were not feeling well last night. The boys have gone to school. You will be alright by the time they return. Come and eat something so you can take some medicine for the pain'. How did he know I had pains? I had tea and bread. He insisted I must eat. This time, the vitamins were not part of the medicine. He also gave me an herb to rub on the sore place. He knew the sore place. I went back to mother's room, squeezed and rubbed the herb around the sore place. The bleeding had gone. There was instant relief and I slept most of the afternoon, in mother's room. When I went back to my room it had been cleaned, the sheets were fresh. That evening my period came.

I did not tell my mother when she returned. She believed I stayed away from school because of my first menstruation. Father welcomed me from school as he had always done and sent us to bed as he had always done but he never gave me any vitamins when I complained of headaches.

Then one day when mother travelled, he asked me as I sat down under the tree picking beans if I had those dreams in the last year. 'No,' I said without looking at him and his newspaper covering his face.

'But you liked the dreams, may be not the last dream.'

I said nothing. That night he came. It was two days after my 14th birthday. I was home on holiday from the boarding school. After diner I complained of a headache. Papa went to the shelf and brought me panadol with the vitamin. I took the panadol but dropped the vitamin on my legs and later in the rubbish bin.

That night I went to bed early but did not sleep. I closed my eyes when I heard the door gently opened. He locked it softly. He walked quietly to the bed, bent down close to my face. I could feel his breathe as he checked whether I had slept. Then he moved away and I opened my eyes and watched him as he removed the towel from his waist and put it on the stool, walked back and knelt down at the foot of my bed. Then he stopped as a door opened. He got up, tied the towel around him and waited by the door. When the other door shut again, he went out.

Early that morning, I went to Aunty Hembadoo's back yard and cut the herb she planted between some banana shrubs and fenced with barbed wire for diseased animals. She had warned that one drop was enough for a cow that needed to be painlessly put to sleep. So I squeezed three in papa's coffee that morning before joining Uncle Daniel whom I had promised to help in the piggery. I was in the pit draining the murky water when Moses ran in to break the news. Uncle Daniel ran off to get his Renault car, his feet bare and covered with dirt. I walked home slowly, and by the time I got there they had left for the hospital. I picked the cup and washed it carefully and put it away.

Mama came back for the burial. She was not a crying woman and that made it easy for everyone. I did not cry. I couldn't even pretend to. I helped mama and my aunties who cooked for those who came to sympathize with mama and papa's brothers.

'He was a good man. He did not deserve to die this young,' one man said.

'And he just got a job after he lost the last one,' another said.

'He loved his children, especially the youngest girl. He was very much concerned with their education. I hope his brothers will not neglect the children,' one said loud to the hearing of the brothers.

I joined my sister in Kaduna after the burial and she and her husband took full responsibility of me and my school. I watched her husband carefully. I locked my door each night and shouted, 'Who is there?' if anyone knocked or tried to open the door. At first my sister was irritated but soon learnt to live with my 'new ways' as she told her husband. Fortunately my sister never travelled and though her husband often looked at my legs, he kept his distance since the day he touched my backside in the kitchen and I told him 'I kill those who do that. If you doubt me ask my father when you get there.' He seemed to read me and concluded I was dangerous. But a few of his friends never tired of chasing me around even to the market. It was not long before I knew the approaches which were common and I knew what to do and say.

The Egyptian had encouraged me to go to the U.K. to study 'on his pocket' after my secondary school. He had made many promises when I would not go near his house. A British Girl whose mother taught in my secondary school had gotten a form for me to apply to her university in London. I was not sure how I would pay my school fees and take care of my needs in London but I had filled the form and given it to her and gotten the admission. I had shown the Egyptian the letter and he had bought my ticket and given me enough money for the school fees for one year and incidental expenses. My friend Alice had told me to tell my mother and my sister I had a scholarship. I had worried about what to say if they asked to see the letter offering me the scholarship but no one asked to see it. The Egyptian had stopped begging as I made arrangements for my trip to the university. I believed he was sure it was definitely going to be easier away from home and so here I was. He had visited twice and once in a while had talked of my lucky star but was really angry the last visit but I did not care.

There was the cinema owner who also saw the star. He was showering me gifts of money and dresses which I saved in an account some other star gazer had opened for me. So when the Egyptian was tired, someone else would be there like this Indian, perhaps…..

HOSPITALITY

AT THE CORNER OF THE Bintang walk, in the Gloria Jean's coffee shop, was a comfortable corner facing the pedestrian crossing. 'Who are Malays here,' Ene asked the American who sat next to her taking a break from his hotel room. 'There are Chinese and Indians here who are Malays. There is a mixture, kind of, not the extreme slant to the eye. It's not easy to tell with the men because they wear the same western clothes but the Muslim women have those small head ties. That's all that distinguishes them. They are not fanatical. The country earns huge money from tourism and they can't afford to dwell on differences like what's ruining fortunate countries like Nigeria.' Ene looked at the man surprised! Did he know she was Nigerian? It was interesting to hear people talk about your country in ignorance of who you were except the Indian traders who were quick to ask if you were Nigerian and quickly lost interest if you were not.

I watched the crowd and envied the small bodied women in small dresses that barely went below their panties and short knickers. Every thing was short and fashionable. Tourists milled by, smoking, chewing or drinking, some alone, some with children, some old men with small Asian girls hanging on to their arms. The men were obviously happy, bending down frequently to smile in the faces of the girls. The girls rarely smiled. I envied their straight kept faces, happy, yet unsmiling. I looked at the American. He looked at me and smiled, 'Are you from Zimbabwe?'

'Yes.' Ene wanted to play along and see where this would lead. Yesterday she was Nigerian and had an unpleasant day with a guy from the Isle of Man who had the impression women from Nigeria when alone were certainly for sale. She had accepted his lunch and half way through he had asked what it would cost him to take her in for three days and if he was satisfied, take her to China for a week. 'I like your body and you are clean and make a good conversation. I can take you out and not feel ashamed. You speak good English,' he had said each sentence between his cigarette and coffee without looking at her.

'Twenty thousand dollars a night,' Ene said looking across the road, sure the man was not a rich man and could not afford the figure she was giving him.

'Twenty K is stiff for nine days don't you think?'

'For a night I said.'

'What gives you the impression you are worth that?'

'O I am worth more than that. That is for you because you don't look like you have much,' Ene said, her eyes still fixed on a couple taking snapshots across the road. He turned to look at her and saw the relaxed ease of her countenance and bold eyes and it dawned on him she was playing a game with him. This was perhaps not a call girl but one could not be sure, he thought. He took out a card from his front chest pocket and dropped it in front of her, getting up in the same instance, 'I am in 209. The name is Streeta.' Ene looked at the card. The hotel was down the road, two blocks from hers. She gathered it with some tissue and pushed it in Streeta's empty coffee mug.

'Ah ah, you look very much like the Congo girls I met in Zimbabwe,' the American was saying with a gentle smile that made him look like a priest. He looked from Ene's eyes to her hands placed flat on the note pad on the table. Both turned to the girls waiting to cross. She wondered if he would have apologized if she had said she was Nigerian following the comments he had made about Nigeria. She was sure he would have said more things, probably said he had been in Nigeria and talk about how hospitable and how corrupt Nigerians were. But now he did not say anything but smile once in a while when their eyes met and looked at the crowd of hurrying bodies and tight faces.

'My name is Blackwater,' he said gently and looked at her fingers.

'My name is Ene,' she said looking at his finger nails, then his crop of black hair that threatened to cover his ears.

'African names usually have a meaning. Does Ene mean something?'

'Mother.'

'That must mean love for mother or mother reborn,' he said almost as if he believed and loved its implications. Ene said nothing.

'So what is mother doing so far away from her family?'

'Holiday.'

'How long?'

'Two weeks.'

'Work?'

'Yes, in a consultancy firm.'

'Married?'

'No.'

'Dating someone serious?'

'No.'

'Otherwise you will not be holidaying alone. I can see you gathering your stuff. Can we meet here tomorrow at lunch time?'

'Why not? Have a pleasant evening."

'You too,' he said calling for another cup of tea.

Ene put the copy of the book she had been reading into her bag and joined the crowd for a walk and window shopping. In front of buildings in the well kept streets, girls, boys, men and women with catalogues called to passersby to come into their beauty palours for feet therapy, body massage – a massage of one part or 4 in one. Ene was tempted and first looked at those having their therapy, quite relaxed in slanting, cushioned chairs. The closest she ever got to that was when she did a pedicure on straight backed chairs.

'Cominn. I will give you a discount, good discount, 20 per cent,' the woman coaxed her. Ene looked at the catalogue and the woman quickly handed it over. Ene flipped through the glossy pictures and the costs which were quite affordable.

'Cominn now,' the woman said again with a smile this time. That won Ene over.

'I will come tomorrow,' she told her and meant it. She looked at the number of the shop. The woman got the message and gave her a card from her apron pocket.

'Si this one, good discount,' another girl said, showing Ene a catalogue but she did not stop this time, to this call or several others in that section of the high street.

There was a lot of food in the streets in the evenings. Ene and Blackwater joined hundreds of families and tourists on plastic chairs and tables, some covered and others bare. They had to raise their voices to hear themselves as everyone chatted gaily or just looked on while waiting for their orders. This reminded Ene of home and the Abuja 'point and kill' parks. The Jalan Alor was all taken up by food kiosks and women and men walked over to you as you passed by with an all in colour menu of delightfully fried, grilled or cooked prawns, shrimps, chicken or frog porridge with noodles or rice. Blackwater had taken her by the hand to show her kioks with the best menu and they had stopped to watch for a while white frogs being cleaned in a large bowl and expertly chopped for preparation to an order. Most of the hotels around Jalon Bintang did not cook. Their occupants ate in the streets or restaurants in the streets nearby. Or you bought your food or fruits and took them to the comfort of your hotel room. This was a busy season and hotel rooms were fully booked. No hotel in the district had a spare room. It was a busy hour and we seized the opportunity of being out early to look out for our favourate meals before settling to an order. After watching the chopped frogs for the fun of it, we ordered a prawn cocktail and grilled fish, rice and a mix of vegetables. All Ene had indulged in since her arrival was shrimps and prawns. Blackwater started with chicken corn soup and an array of chop suyi, ram in some source crowning his noodles. He seemed to love food, Ene thought as she watched him empty the plate and pick the bowl of fruit salad.

'You are quiet,' he said with that priestly smile. But Ene would not tell him that she had come out late because she was on the computer for two hours with friends on the net catching up with recent bombings of police stations and public places back home. The updates were not pleasant and Ene had lost some appetite but had to eat because it was now 6.20 and she had not eaten a meal since the coffee at Gloria Jean at about 11 which was her breakfast and lunch. She had been lost in Abubakar Gimba's Once Upon a Reed and some scriblings in her notebook. If she did not eat now Blackwater would be disappointed and she would be hungry all night.

Ene loved prawns and these were huge ones beautifully encased in lovely cream. Though Ene avoided creamy foods she was determined to enjoy everything she had avoided this holiday but she had no idea her grilled fish would come with fresh black pepper. In Nigeria ground black pepper was cooked as a spice. Here it came fresh and mixed with the food and Ene had chewed into a good number before she realized what it was. She lost her appetite after chewing the black pepper and drank orange juice till the taste was off her teeth and tongue. She carefully picked and ate the fish and drank more orange juice. A couple looked at her and Blackwater and talked fast. He looked at them and smiled. 'They must be wondering…a black woman and white man.' Then he placed his hand on hers on the table and asked if she enjoyed the food.

'Yes but the black peper almost ruined it. At home we use it as a spice not chewed fresh.' She winced. He smiled sympathetically and helped her out of her seat.

The woman looked at the unfinished food as she collected her money and asked if Ene had finished and she said yes. Did she want the fish wrapped to take away? She said no.

'You don't like the food?' she asked. Ene told her the meal was great.

'But you no eat,' she insisted Ene should eat more. Ene smiled and as they left she remembered Diouf in Senegal where she had left the Pullman Hotel Dakar in search of a Nigerian meal. In company of the friendly Diouf, they had found a place with the bitter leaf soup he liked and which she also liked. But there was neither eba nor pounded yam. They had to make do with ground rice. The Senegalese were best at tourism and fashion in place of farming. The ground rice was smooth but hard but they sure enjoyed it after days of tea, bread, rice, or spaghetti and salad at the hotel.

After the mound of ground rice and bitterleaf soup in the Nigerian restaurant in Senegal Diouf and Ene had walked into the evening sun. She was rather heavy when they stepped out of the restaurant. Her escort joked that he hoped she would not sink into the sandy short routes they picked as she insisted they walk to the high way for some exercise before taking a taxi. She had made a mistake of wearing some heeled shoes. People around her were all in flats. Her heels sank in as she walked and each step had to be pulled out of the sand with some force.

'There is so much sand here, how do you farm?'

'There is no farm. Who wants to farm anyway? Little rain, hard work.'

'But you are surrounded by water.'

'And the marabouts do not want water, so no rain.'

She wondered if the marabouts could really stop rains. She smiled remembering the story of a witch who was taken to court for killing a neighbor with lightening. She could not perform her witchcraft of calling down lightening 'because it was not raining,' she had told the magistrate. Ene could see why buildings here had no roofing sheets. The roofs served as laundries. They had little rain to worry about while the sea roared all around them and men hawked tea and coffee in the streets from large kettles in small disposable cups. She smiled.

'Am I missing out on something?' Blackwater asked. She told him the story of the witch who could not invoke lightening in court because it did not rain.

'So the court could not convict her for lack of evidence.'

'Even though she agreed with her accusers she was a witch.'

'Why did you think of that now?'

'The judge happens to be a friend I have a lot of respect for and there is something in your smile that reminds me of him, something naughty yet serious.' They laughed.

'You want to have a drink?' he asked.

'Not now. Perhaps some other time.'

'Tomorrow then.' He walked her to the reception of her hotel and wished her a good night but did not leave until she was in the lift.

The Senegalese experience was different from the Bintang high street coffee shop where she watched the dual deck buses called London buses back home. Unlike the red London buses, these were green and white with red and blue strips, others in green and yellow, red and white with brands of the different owners. The buses all looked new with fresh paints, new tyres. Ene made a point to visit the Indian caves in one of these buses and she did the next day with Blackwater. The passengers were more aggressive than the Senagalese and their French tourists. In Dakar no one went round checking tickets like in Kuala Lumpur where passengers' tickets were not only checked but the man checking tickets also had to shout on two occasions at two girls, 'No eating on the bus.' The scenery to the caves was breath taking. She wondered if the forests were real or man-made. She had often heard that palm forests here came from Nigeria. Nothing seemed impossible here.

Ene ordered coffee and sipped, watching a Caucasian couple take some photographs of each other under the lighted palm tree. The trees lit up the city both night and day and Ene thought this was why people rarely slept here and perhaps why they walked about all day and night. The couple then asked a boy waiting for the light to take a picture of them beside one of the buses. He grabbed the camera, gave them a quick shot and thrust the camera at them and ran across as the green light came on and the bus pulled away. She sensed Blackwater seat next to her and she turned around and smiled her greetings. He smiled in reply. 'How was the night and morning?' She nodded and spread out her arms. 'Very well. And you?'

'Great. I had a long walk but still want to walk to the twin towers this evening. Join me?'

'Ah great. I was thinking of walking there this evening! That's a beautiful coincidence!'

'Great. Coffee?'

'Green tea.' He went to make the orders.

It was Saturday and Ene remembered the next day would be Sunday. There was no catholic church around here. Ene recalled the high street in Dakar a stone throw from the Presidential Villa. There were a few security men by the roadside helping pedestrians cross. A good number of people were going in and out of a casino close by owned by Lebanese business men. Right across the road opposite the casino was a Catholic Church where a few tourists were taking pictures. But the street wasn't this busy and if you stopped to wait for the bus in front of the casino opposite the church, you could see some tourists taking pictures unhurriedly under the statues of La Vierge Marie Merc de Jesus Le Sauveur which looked gracefully, prayerfull upon them. Ene had attended mass in a Chapel at the Goree Island where slave dealers had prayed. There were six people in attendance. Ene considered herself lucky to have arrived there just as mass was starting and joined in. Every building on the island was stone, metal and concrete. It was solid, unpenetratable with high, smooth stone walls looking down sea level. French tourists walked around pursued by hawkers with souvenirs. Some tourists sat with artists and talked quietly. Ene didn't like heights and looking down that wall made her queasy; so the chapel had offered some relief. Her escort was a Muslim but waited a short walk from the chapel. He took her to the hall where slaves awaited shipment. It looked like the baggage collection point at Murtala Mohammed Airport. Ene turned on her heels and her escort followed. He said later that he was sure she was upset at the thought of what the captives went through. He said he felt the same even though he had come there so many times and said he was sure he would have jumped into the sea from those walls if he had been a victim..

Blackwater came back with the tea on a tray and set it in front of Ene

'What's the matter? You look like you've seen some ghosts!' he exclaimed.

Ene smiled. She had no idea the thoughts of that Island would get her so upset and felt like she could kill someone. Blackwater looked at her briefly and asked her to take her tea.

'Someone must have hurt you real bad the way you look.'

'No, not me but someone was hurt real bad and I just recalled it.'

'I am sorry.'

'Yeah.'

They remained quiet for a while looking into the street and thinking their different thoughts. After a while Blackwater looked at her hands on the table and put his palm on them. 'You have lovely hands.'

'Yeah. Thanks,' she said, an afterthought.

'What are you writing? I watched you for a while from Starbucks. Sometimes I thought you saw me. You looked directly at me and then went back to your scribbling and it was not long before I realized you were looking at a scenario in your mind's eye. That must be a wonderful story.'

'I hope it will be as good as you think.' She looked at her watch. 'I won't be a moment. Just hang on for me,' she said and hurried off before the man would offer to walk her to the hotel. She would drop her bag and notes and wear comfortable shoes. She passed the building she was told served as a church for all denominations. On arrival in Kuala Lumpur she could not find a church and when she found one it was a multi worship centre. She was not sure when she would find an acceptable familiar group of worshipers and so stayed away. First Christmas in her life she could remember not being at mass. First time she said mass using the Buletin she had packed for the trip. It went well except she had no bread and so Ene went down to a shop and got a small bottle of wine and bread. Who said she could not call on God to change that bread and wine into His body and blood? Who could say it was not changed. That night Ene had a real meal as Christ had done with his apostles, not the flat paste she had on her tongue every mass. She slept well, happy that she had a better alternative to a multy worship church.

In about fifteen minutes she was back with a small purse for her phone. She sat down and gave Blackwater a wide cheery smile. He was looking at a girl crossing in haste to beat the light and almost toppled on the pavement. Her left heel had broken off as she rushed to cross over. She stepped up and took a seat next to Ene after looking around in vain for an alternative seat. Ene was used to seeing Asians avoiding seats on the same table or next to her which was alright. It saved her the loud talks which she didn't understand and which distracted her thoughts. Ene smiled at the girl and she smiled weakly and looked worriedly at the shoe in her hand, put it on the floor and took off the second, looking at the heel. 'You can knock off the heel,' Ene said demonstrating with her hands in case she did not speak English.

'Ah gud, tank you,' she said and bent over, knocked off the second heel, put both heels in a plastic bag and slipped her feet in the now flat shoes. She walked carefully over to the counter testing the shoes, bought a cup of ice cream and returned to her chair more confident.

'Tank you, tank you,' she said again and sat down. Ene smiled again. She was amused because back home it was a general assumption that only Abba shoes dropped off heels.

This young Malay woman certainly did not buy her shoes in Nigeria.

Blackwater smiled and stood up, checked his back pocket for his passport and pointed to a shop across the road. 'I will be back shortly,' he said to Ene and headed for the crossing where a few people were waiting. The success of tourism here could be seen in the licensed money changers in the streets. Within a radius of 50 meters where she sat were over ten of them. From where Ene sat she could count five 'money changers,' then the cameras and photographs being taken at the corners, at the pedestrian crossing, under the lighted palm trees, in the coffee shop all attested to the large number of tourists.

On Christmas day, a few people wearing the Fr. Xmas caps they had been coerced to buy the previous day in the streets by aggressive traders milled by. Others were shopping. Ene had warned herself to be carefull when she bought things from the Indian traders who would first ask where you came from and then triple the cost when they heard you were Nigerian. They would say Nigerians had money. Well, that seemed to be the case every where you went because the Nigerians they talked about were the politicians and their children and of course the traders who bought anything from plastics to cars.

Ene watched the woman with broken heels for a while licking the ice-cream and then turned her attention to Blackwater counting some money just handed to him across the counter. There was hardly any difference between Christmas eve, Christmas day and any other day. The shops remained open and busy, people shopping or simply sightseeing. The girl who did the paper work in the coffee shop pulled a chair nearby and smiled at Ene with a nod. She did that every day and earlier she would have called to one of the boys behind the counter to serve her. She never ate the food from the counter. She brought her meals in a bag and for a week Ene watched her unpack her lunch from a bag, push the papers aside and focus on her little bowls for about twenty minutes, peering at a paper in between her swallows. That was the difference between KL and Dakar where such employees would eat from the counter as soon as they had served their customers and their attention was not needed. And Ene missed the 'bon apetit.'

Blackwater returned. 'Shall we?'

Ene got up, said good bye to the broken heeled girl with a speck of ice cream on her pink blouse who repeated 'tank you.' As they walked along to the Twin Towers Ene looked keenly for a familiar face among oncoming black faces in the crowd. Four days earlier, bent over her notebook, she had heard familiar tones of voices. She had listened. They were Igbo guys interspersing their conversation with English words, 'Its business!' one said tightly to the other two. She turned to take a view of them. They looked away and talked. One wore a white shirt with Paris printed boldly in front. He said, 'Look, I am not like him with family that send him money. And my friend in immigration has to be paid to regularize his visa. If he goes home he can get it done but he should weigh the cost of ticket. It will cost him about 400k this busy season. I am asking him for 120k. I give 50k to the man at the immigration. And it is becoming more difficult now. See de way dis people jus wake up and make new laws. At the airport dey focus on Nigerians while odas pass witout a single search.'

'That's not our business but if you look around our boys have become bad boys. And the overstay charges are especially targeted at us. Any way, with my Liberian passport I am saturated,' said the second who grabbed his phone and began to talk in that peculiar way common with traders. When he wanted to talk he would take the ear piece to his lips and then return it to his ear as he listened and then back to his lips as he talked. Then he placed it on his pack of cigarettes and continued the business discussion, expressive in the movement of hands, head, shoulders and face. Blackwater took Ene's hand as they got to a crossing. She watched in admiration a pretty half naked girl waiting to cross and she remembered the girl from her red and yellow dyed hair at the coffee shop four days earlier. Ene was looking at her when she heard one of the four Nigerians ask her, 'Is anyone here? Can I sit?'

Ene looked up at him still talking on the phone in Igbo. After standing over her for the period of his conversation he sat down, looked at her.

'You are Nigerian,' Ene said

'Yes. And you?'

'Nigerian'

'From where?' She told him a lie and added, 'I live in Abuja.'

'I live in Abuja too. In Karu. I have my house there,' he said.

Ene told him where she lived and where she worked.

'I am a business man in fashion and electronics. I was in Indonesia. They have the best in fashion. I had to come here. It's a long story.' He shook his head.

'We can sum up long stories,' Ene said kindly.

'Yes. My girl friend who use to shortie me refused to. She say she can get my goods from the companies any where and even pay for it but I should not return.'

Ene asked the why with her eyes.

'I know it is one of my friend.'

'Mmm?'

'He told her things about me. Yes. In fact when I call my friends now they are avoiding talking to me about her. One of them was close enough to tell me, "Ask the person who is driving your car," so you see, he told my girl that I was planning to take her home if we marry. She believed because I had told her once, even two times that we will go home. How can I marry and not take my wife home? He used it against me. The girls there hear bad things about our country and they do not want to come home with us.'

'Ah that's not a good friend,' I said kindly.

'But I have a spirit that use to make people say I have something, you know. If I supply goods to anyone, I will go early and wait before they open the shop, then I will chatt with the young man opening the shop. You know when people are happy as they start market, it will be good. So I will ask him why he is early and looking cool. He must just be coming from his woman. And he will start laughing even as he is opening the shop. Then I will go in and help him flip dust from the shelves and leave. The whole, day, sales will be too much for him. One day the oga even came early to see what I do. He believed I had something. He met me and I said funny things to him which made him laugh and I left. Within a week I will get all my money and leave. Now he complains that I don't come again, and market is low.'

I smiled. He told an Indian Malay, who was looking at him all the time he talked to stop looking at him. The girl looked away. Five women walked by chatting gaily. Three of them were Muslims from their small beautiful scarves of blue and black, pink and purple. The other two wore orange shorts and a green blouse and white shorts and a poker dotted blouse. Once in a while purple hat fed the man on her left with a straw and then sucked on the same straw before turning to her friends who were talking at the same time. They talked in Chinese Malay and often stopped to listen to the blue jeans, blue and white scarf who spoke loudly whenever she wanted attention. They laughed and seemed happy. The Indonesian deportee was talking but Ene half listened, saturated with the beauty around her and then the news on the screen to her left with pictures of the bombings of the catholic church in Madalla, Abuja. The number of the dead as usual was uncertain. She looked sadly at the picture of a dead girl being carried out of the church, the flared dress leaving much of her thighs exposed indecently. Ene looked away. The guy kept talking, not unconcerned with the news.

'My name is Chinedu,'

'Ene.'

'You have beautiful hands.'

'So how did you come here?' Ene asked to draw attention away from her hands.

'Dat is a good question. I have a friend in the U.S. I called Ayo and told him what I was in. How some one listened to my conversation on phone and forge and collect my goods. I was talking to my sister. Someone heard us and went to clear the goods pretending dat he is Chinedu.'

'Oh that must have been terrible for you.'

'Ayo came two days later. I just got a call and it was him. He said, 'I am here'. I was able to get out to this place. If I can get like two thousand dollars, I will sort out myself.'

'You don't have a visa?'

'No. But no one ask me for my Identity since I came here. If you dress well, Nigerians here dress anyhow, with slippers. I was just telling one how he can get to me here trough safe roads. You see dis white trouser I am wearing. It has a jacket. It is only now you see me in just this shirt but every ting has to be executive. I am into fashion. One elderly woman in Indonesia, she is Hausa, told me to get papers trough her. She said when we return she will get me job as assistant to her governor. But I can't marry her. Even when she invite me to tea I look for excuse.'

'Why?'

'You see, if she is like ten-twelve years older dan me, I won't care. After all, my parents are not alive anymore and I will tell anyone to go to hell. But you see if you are forty, that woman is sixty-five. I don't want trouble.'

'Mm, I guess you are right.'

'So you are a consultant teacher. Have you tried business?'

'I am not a business person. I like where I am.'

'So when did you come here? You know dey don't pay teachers well in Nigeria and I hear promotion depend on goodwill and somebody can seat on your promotion as long as he like or is in charge. You can't go on like dat. And you need to do someting to support dat salary.'

'Almost a week now. Will leave next week. I was at the university two days ago to see some boys whose parents sent messages to. I am surprised they sent so many things. And all those things are here. One even sent cabin biscuits. And food is so cheap here. See every where people are eating. I couldn't eat the first two days I was here. And one of the boys said he was eating once a day so I had to get him money. He can't open an account yet so his parents can't send him money.' Ene said looking away from the TV.

'But I can give you my account number for them. I have an international credit card.' He showed me the card. 'And they are lucky they can eat once a day. I hope you don't mind if I ask you. Are you married?'

'No.'

'I am not one who takes weeks, months to know I love someone. You are beautiful. Plenty of hair. I like hair in women. You are very pretty.'

'Every woman is pretty.' Ene wanted to add that especially first meeting or when she is needed for quick money but didn't. She looked at the thickening traffic.

'No. You are warm. I like your voice….' He was not sure of what to say.

'Let's go to the Twin Towers.' Ene checked time on the mobile.

'Wait for me here. Let me send a message at the cyber café.'

'Let me go and sit with you,' he offered.

'No. You wait for me,' she said, getting up.

'Ok,' he said in a resigned tone.

Ene went to her hotel a short distance away. She dropped her bag on the bed, changed her shoes. She knew where The Towers were and it was better in the evenings. She preferred to walk.

She was back in twenty minutes. They walked and he talked. He told her about his business, his brother in Canada with whom he was enstranged because his brother was told he was mixed up with his woman. And his brother heard he was ritualistic and would get rid of him to take his properties and money and wife. He told Ene about relations who had gone home this Christmas to marry on credit and the frauds at their weddings this December. He talked about those who had bought expensive cars to show they were big boys, but would regret shortly after.

They did some window shopping and he seemed uncomfortable with the items Ene picked. He wondered why anyone would buy a bra Ene had just looked at for N7,000. He picked a pair of slippers and asked Ene what it would cost back home in Abuja. She told him she was the wrong person to ask about costs. She had no idea. She rarely wore things like that. It was too silvery and decorative. He agreed and asked if she could take a bag of shoes for his brother. 'When leaving,' she said, if she didn't have much luggage. Ene thought of the things that could be in the bags.

'I will go to the airport with you and pay if they charge for any extra,' he said quickly

When they were through at the Towers she told him it was time to leave. He wanted to sit down, play. She said she had some work to do. She had come here to rest but also to write and had organized time. He wanted them to take a taxi. She said she wanted to walk. He noted she was atletic. It was a long walk back. Ene was tired but satisfied with the day. She had to call home. She had to do an hour on the internet, have dinner and take a bath. Bed was usually one-two a.m for her. And she had to close this chapter by refusing to give her phone number.

The next day she moved over to a Chinese eatery to change her diet to a vegetable, sugar free cakes and green tea and away from Chinedu.

'What is on your thoughts? You are supposed to be on holiday,' Blackwater pulled her closer crossing the road at a no crossing point. She ran with him to a Peugeot car shop. 'You like the new 408?'

'I still prefer the 407,' Ene said.

'You talk like you have one.'

'Yes I do have one.'

'How old?'

'Four years.'

'What car would you want in place of the Peugeot?'

'A Tundra.'

'What do you want that for?'

'Ah look at the lights!' Ene exclaimed reclaiming her left hand and running ahead.

Blackwater took her to some steps where a few people had sat waiting for the lights and Ene gladly sat down.

'I will be back shortly,' said Blackwater and ran towards the high building. Ene was sure he had gone to pick some drinks.

She did not want any sugary drinks which was one reason she had moved to the Chinese outfit across the road from Starbucks. The first day there was taken up by interesting tourists. She had watched a Caucasian couple and their teenage children walk by, the father and son in front, the mother and daughter behind holding hands, the girl with her father's blond hair, the boy with his mother's hazzle brown and her upturned lips. She could not help smiling. They stopped by one of the tall palm trees that lined up the street to take a photograph. The girl smiled with a lift of the lips similar to her father's full lips and beautiful set of teeth. Ene smiled widely at the resemblances of mother and son and father and daughter. As if reading her thoughts, the woman smiled back with a wave of the hand. She waved back.

Two elderly Caucasian women hobbled up to them, the woman stepped in between them and the man took a shot. The teenagers stood on both sides of the two elderly ladies and the man took another shot. The boy took the camera from his father and the man joined the women and he took a shot with one of the elderly women. They moved on again in that order, father and son, mother and daughter hanging onto her arm and the distance gradually created between the older and younger. The elderly women talked to each other in loud tones especially when the traffic increased, holding an ear to the other. They both frowned at a young boy who stopped in front of them to ask for money.

The boy hissed at them and walked over to Ene's table asking for money. She waved him away but he was stubborn and insisted she gave him something. One of the two men sitting on the next table asked him in Arabic to leave. He shouted back that he was not begging them. The man said Ene was his wife, the boy was not to disturb her. The boy shouted some abuses and the second man got up and pulled back his chair. The boy ran off but stopped a short distance away as the man sat down and shouted what seemed like some obscenities and walked away. The man who had said

Ene was his wife turned to her and asked her to join them at their table. She told him she was comfortable where she was.

'He is crazy,' he said

'Every four people on the street are crazy,' Ene replied

'Four!' He showed four fingers.

'Yes. That's what a British survey said several years back. It may be worse now,' Ene said.

'You are from?'

'Nigeria.'

'I am also from Africa'

'Which country?'

'Tunisia, Africa.'

'Yea.'

'I like your dress. Beautiful'. Ene nodded. That morning she came out in the common Nigerian long skirt and stylish blouses and the head piece which she draped on her neck. A Sudanese lady had salaamed her and she had salaamed back. She had noted Ene must be a Nigerian and Ene had happily concorded and asked her where she came from. 'Sudan,' she replied. She then asked if Ene was a student. Many people had asked her that question and each time she told them she was a teacher, they appreciated her. The Sudanese did the same as she moved closer to her and they chatted until they parted ways at Times Square building which hosted a hotel and the University of Hospitality.

Ene wanted to see the courses such a university offered. She wasn't surprised to find such a university here, a country that earned a large budget from tourism. She spent an hour there, shown round by a guy who concluded Ene would not come to Malaysia without visiting the islands or the caves to see some Indian culture. He was free today and offered to take her to Kenting. He wanted to show her some Malay hospitality. It reminded her again of Dakar where someone offered every day to take her to some sights, or a market or a tailor. Tailoring was big businesess in Senegal. Ene had seen Nigerian traders displaying some designs usually referred to as Senegalese but it had never made an impact until her visit. She did not get this hospitality in Spain or South Africa where each time she went out someone thought she was hawking her body. She did not get this hospitality in Cape Town but had some in Johanesbourgh. She liked the South African women; Lindiwe, Mantsha, Menkita were wonderful. They took her to see Mandela's house and they had tea in his daughter's restaurant which reminded her of New Delhi's Appollo Hospital. But no, in India people were hospitable only when you were interested in something of a profit, Ene thought. At the Mandela house they ran around taking photographs with those lovely women who wanted nothing. No one chased them as they took photographs in front of the house! No police or soldiers. No guns!

Blackwater sat next to her and she could feel his warmth but most people were standing and shouting at the brilliance of lights and spray of showers and they stood up to join the crowd. The excitement ran through her like the fireworks and water sprays that enveloped the lghts. It was heavenly and she didn't know when she started shouting to the Abba tune that rendered the air and before long the chorus filled the space. As they left Ene wondered if she could walk the distance to the hotel. But as if reading her thoughts Blackwater said a taxi was waiting on the other side and gently pulled her along.

She was sleepy but like with the guide at the University of Hospitality she struggled to stay awake. On that day she had not dared close her eyes the whole one hour fifteen minutes bus ride to Kenting Highlands. Her escort repeated a second time that this mesmerizing country was only 50 years old. A year younger than her own country, Ene thought, yet everything was old, run down. Well everything here was new, much newer than the 50 years but she was ushered into the skyway as it was called and they headed up the mountain passing returning skyways with laughing or newspaper reading occupants. She couldn't do any of the two. She couldn't even drink the canned drink she had bought at the boarding terminal, as she looked down the valleys and gullies and rocks and streams and forests below her. Then she'd look up at the oncoming 'skyways' sliding down and hers sliding up with no drivers. The two would go pass and someone would try to take a photograph of the next one but by the time the camera clicked it was the bushes and trees and rocks that registered. Then the next and the next. There were over a hundred of them picking thousands of fun seekers queuing patiently on each side. There were no delays and lights never went off! Imagine the skyway stopping mid air because lights had gone off!

Kenting was amazing. The casino was huge and her escort was a keen gambler. He said there was something for everyone on the tables or machines. Ene gave him RM50. He lost and asked if she would play as women had luck. She said no. There was a floor for children, computer animation and they went for the wild games –boxing, wrestling, fights. There were the hotels-Starbuck, First world hotel, Theme Hotel with a Theme entertainment and out there and in the lakes were the water games, the boats. Ene's feet were aching. She had on the wrong shoes. Kenting was not something you saw in one day. She was told the owner was dead but cars still came 3 times every day to move money. The man had two sons and he had left a name and huge employment opportunities for the youth of his country and the government had supported him with that dual carriage way up the mountain and the skyway. He had promised his government he would bring presidents to that country and he had made the mountain a home of hospitality to which thousands including presidents trooped daily, happily spending their money.

They drove away and Ene watched the twin towers blaze behind the fire works. It was a city of the night of lights and Ene thought, 'No one sleeps because there is always light.' It reminded her of ST. Peter's Basilica at the Vatican where she saw the lights with her eyes closed. 'Here we are,' Blackwater said and Ene realized she had slept off her head on his arm.

'Thank you. This was a beautiful night I won't forget.' As she turned to go, Blackwater handed her a little red box. This must be why he went to the Money Changer and why he left her under the lights, Ene thought. She took the box and walked to the lift and up to her room.

It was 8am and Ene had been on her computer for an hour when she remembered the red box. It sat next to the bedside lamp, imposing. She got up, walked over to the bed, sat down and picked the box. She examined it and tried to guess what could be in it. There was a trade mark but she was familiar with only a few brands. She opened it, careful not to hurt her nail. It was a lovely wrist watch and as she lifted it out she saw the most beautiful gold bracelet she ever laid claim to. She put the wrist watch down, picked the bracelet and slipped it on her wrist. It fitted perfectly and so did the watch. He must have somehow taken measurement of her wrist, all those times he took her hand or placed his palms on them, Ene thought. For a while she wondered why he bought her these expensive gifts. They were tourists who would go their own way after some days. There was no intimacy, no promises, just politeness and thin but encouraging smiles on his part. She wondered if she should reject the gifts, but she had already accepted them and she hoped there would be no demands. She returned the bracelet and wristwatch to the red box and put it in her travel case and returned to her computer on the table.

That day she did not go to Gloria's Coffee bar. She had carrots and bananas with green tea and worked on her computer till 3pm, then had a shower and went for lunch in an Indian restaurant two streets from her hotel. She had rice and ram cooked in a tasty source with a glass of fresh orange juice and returned to the hotel. She bought a bottle of red wine and cashew nuts. She had no plans to go out again for what was left of the day. She stopped over at another Indian shop to top up her call card and spent an hour that evening talking with family members and friends back home. Everyone she spoke to knew someone who knew someone who died in the Boko Haram bombings in Jos and Madalla. People were afraid to go to church, they said. The next day would be New Year eve. Ene had been looking forward to the fireworks but the news from home dimmed the excitement. Something seemed clipped away from the heights of her vacation. Would she also stay away from church when she returned home? It was unthinkable.

What was life without one hour of walkout and an hour of worship every morning which crowned her day? What was worship without a Christian family with whom you sang songs of praise and thanksgiving? She laid down on the floor and read Helon Habila's Oil on Water but it made her feel no better. She looked at Achebe's Anthills and decided it was the wrong book to read at that moment of tumult. She turned on the TV and searched the channels. She stopped at The Saint of a Woman which had just started, got up and made herself comfortable under the beddings. It was just what she needed at this moment, some love story.

At 9am Ene went to Starbucks and had coffee. A couple joined her on the table arguing. It took a while before she turned her attention to them, still flipping through a magazine she had picked at the Indian shop. The woman was saying with a murderous look, 'How could you even imagine that?'

'How did he know we were here, calling you on a number you picked up yesterday?'

'His sister. I sent her my number. Got my number from his sister and wanted to know how we were doing. For God's sake William! I don't think this relationship is going to work. I think we should go back tomorrow. I am going to call the airline and if you are not leaving I will.'

'You can't stay away from him?'

'Shit!' she said and got up, grabbed her bag and walked out. Williams remained where he was. Ene flipped a page and looked up right into Williams eye. He looked into her eyes.

'She is lying,' he said. 'Last night she called him in the toilet. She called him sweetheart. She didn't know I was right by the door and she said she missed him tons!'

Ene waved to Blackwater who was looking at her through the half glazed glass panes. Williams followed her gaze. 'And there you are with a regular. I hope you are not cheating on someone away from home,' he said picking up his cap. Williams walked past Blackwater with a nod. Blackwater remained where he was for a while, then walked in and sat on the seat the woman had vacated.

'What was he saying to you?'

'That his fiancée was cheating on him and hoped I was not cheating away from home.' Ene did not tell him Williams said he was a regular.

'Don't let him spoil a lovely day with his problem. We have to prioritize our lives.' And he philosophized for a while on the happiness of life and choices.

Thanks for the red box. Everything there was beautiful. I was not expecting anything from you. That's very kind of you.' Ene looked at her hands. She thought she should have worn them so he could see how good they looked on her.

'We will have lunch and then you will go get some sleep and get ready for the long evening. New Year eve is a night to remember here and New Year, tomorrow, has something special for you, something you will love and remember me for. Rememberances are the non object tools that keep life in motion. Let's go now.'

It was 1pm when Ene opened her eyes and sprang out of bed. She was unsure which to do first, pick the paper under the door or go to urinate. She picked the paper and ran into the toilet reading it as she urinated. Her mouth fell open. 'Ene I had to leave for Doha unexpectedly. You were sleeping soundly I was sure because you went to bed about 5 this morning. You have a Tundra waiting to be shipped and since I don't have your address, you will call the following number or email them the details for the shipment. They will call you when the baggage arrives. Then you may call or email the following address to say thank you and if you want me to visit Congo, I will.' It was simply signed Blackwater. Ene wiped her face to be sure she was not dreaming. She remembered the night of fireworks and sparkles at midnight, the shouts and screams of teen and twenties at what was the name of that square? She was sure she would not remember anything for now but she could remember telling Blackwater she liked the Tundra. What was wrong with the man? Ene wondered.

Ene went to the other side of the bed and sat facing the window. She looked at the paper and read the message again. There was a phone number and an email but no address. She called the number. A voice confirmed there was a Tundra for an Ene who would supply her details for shipping to her country. Could she see the wagon? She had asked. 'Sure why not,' the voice had said and given an address not far from the Twin Towers. She went there, saw the wagon, looked it over and furnished them with her address. She went to the hotel Blackwwater had mentioned and asked for him at the reception. 'Ah yes Blackwater checked out this morning,' the young man said, his face still down. Was this real. This was the first time a man would love her this much without wanting anything. She thought. It was puzzling.

Ene had a friend in the customs who called to tell her the car was ready for collection. She went to Lagos to clear the wagon and got a driver to drive it to Abuja. She got the car registered the next day and sent an email to the address Blackwater had written down. There was no response. She had wondered several times if she were to tell him she was Nigerian and not Congolese. She called the number but it was switched off. She sent another mail that Sunday just before leaving for Uchenna's house for lunch. She had promised the three boys a ride to the amusement park. On the way the three terrors had a rod with a pointed end which they threatened each other with and pricked the roof in several places and Ene said she would put them in a taxi. They quietened and sat down for the rest of the trip. When they were busy at play she went back to inspect the pricks and jabs the car had suffered at the hands of the boys. She robbed a bad spot with her finger and a white powdery substance appeared on her finger. She tapped it again and the powder trickled on the black leather seat.

Ene looked at the tough plastic cover round the leathered roof and stepped out of the wagon, thoughtful. She went to her bag and picked a nail cutter which contained a pen knife and returned to the back seat, tore off the plastic dust and dirt covering and ran her palm on the roof. It was smooth but hard. She tapped round the prick and the powder trickled out on her finger. She put her finger to her nose. She had been introduced to drug substances at the psychiatric home the St. Vincent de Paul committee of her church visited weekly. People used to be checked as they came in because some of the rich kids put there for rehabilitation paid pushers to smuggle in bits for them. These were put in a counter and a guard had shown them and even encouraged them to taste it. Ene had smelt and tasted it a few times and knew right away what she had in her wagon. She called her brother.

Thursday afternoon Ene returned to her office from a late lunch and almost bumped into Blackwater who was about to leave. The secretary had told him she was not sure if Ene would return to the office. It was rather late she had said. Ene gave him a surprised wide smile and Blckwater gathered her in a bear hug. They walked into her office holding hands.

'You must be surprised to see me,' he said chukling.

'Not exactly. I was sure you would get my details from the car dealers.' Ene replied coyly.

'Well that. But I knew you were Nigerian the first day I met you. I had watched you talking to some Nigerian guys the day before and exchanging views. You were particularly upset about some bombing of a church.'

'Yes. You were there. I did not notice you at all.'

'I got your message. I am glad you like your wagon. I expected to see it as I drove into your parking lot in a cab,' he said. What he did not tell her was that he had a key and had simply intended to move the car away to a planned destination, off load the contents and dump it where she could find it.

'Yes but that happiness didn't last.' She pulled out a drawer to her right and handed him the police report of the stolen wagon at the amusement park four days earlier with all original papers, just two days after registration. What she did not tell him was that she had spent over an hour flushing cocaine worth ten wagons down her toilet and burning the wraps in the street with the rubbish that had not been collected in a week. She did not tell him that the papers had been changed and the car was now ash colour instead of black and it was traded for a Hilux in Cotonu.

Rather she said, 'The police are sure to find it.' Blackwater looked at her for a while with what he hoped she would see as sympathy for her loss and then got up. 'I must get to my hotel at once. I will call you. Let me know when the police find your wagon.' And before Ene could go round her desk to walk him out, he was gone.

THE POLITICIAN'S PROMISE

ABOJE WAS UP EARLY THAT morning, took his bath and had an unusual early breakfast. Like him, he was sure many would come out early on this first day to avoid the last minute rush. In the last two elections he had not bothered to vote. It was common knowledge that nobody's vote counted. Many working class civil servants like him did not waste their time queuing on lines with women and traders to cast votes for people who with good intentions for the people had no chance against the intrigues of box snatching and thumb printing for the selected candidates. But this was different. For the first time, they were told, not even zoning mattered. Candidates would be voted on merit irrespective of where they came from and here was a minority candidate. It was not just that the candidate was a minority from a poverty stricken place like his but that he had a background he was sure would play a significant role in at least the country's infrastructure. No one needed a degree to know how much poverty could be reduced with regular electricity and good roads.

'I am here.' He recognized Ameh's voice as he called out to him.

'Will be with you shortly.' Aboje put his face out through the window, waved and hurried back into the room for his sandals. In a minute he was out.

'How was the night?' He shook Ameh's hand.

'Not bad. Your family? I told mine I will call them when I see what we have to go through.'

'The same. We hope for the best but no chances. Everyone in my house is voting except the underaged. And not just my house. With the exception of diehards in my street, every one of age is voting for our candidate.'

'In fact, the same thing in my ministry. For the first time, party has no play in this election. The same thing in the church.'

'Aha! It is not just the church. Even our Muslim brothers.'

Aboje and Ameh agreed to walk down considering the short distance and good weather. They were pleased to see dozens of groups here and there talking excitedely. Two men were talking out of a queue waiting to write names on a sheet of paper. The registration officers had not yet arrived but someone had quickly produced a notebook to beat the rush and keep people in line.

Aboje listened to the two men.

'You will vote for this man?' the bald-headed man asked.

'I will vote for his agenda. It seems credible. At least one which if he puts in place, the others will naturally follow up,' his tall light skinned partner said confidently.

'The roads? They all say they will fix the roads but the roads are where the big contracts are made.'

'Not the roads, silly.......'

'Of course, the rails! They will put back those ancient tracks and coaches for us to use while they run around in helicopters and private planes.'

'Not exactly but the trains will do much in curtailing the cost of transporting both food and petroleum products.'

'And what of the powerful cabal who own the trucks that crashed the railways. They are very much alive and want more money to compete with the Bill Gates et al.'

'You need not worry about this cabal thing. It is an excuse of unproductive critics.'

'O water then, we are right here in the capital, a new city and you live in the largest estate any city has built anywhere. It's a town in itself with no tap water. A few wealthy people who live there dug bore holes from where water vendors buy. The rest depend on *mai ruwa*, the vendors, who sell a jerry can of water for twenty naira when light is steady and fifty when light is gone for one week or more. People resort to very unpleasant behavior. My neighbor, Florence, called in the police to report a family on the third floor of her building who resorted to throwing shit in plastic bags down her backyard where Florence does her laundry. The police came to inspect, found the allegations true even though the woman on the third floor kept denying. The police asked my neighbor if she wanted to go to court. She said not this time but she would if that situation repeated itself.'

'Well, here we are registering to choose a president who like others never had shoes while going to school in his village. Maybe I will stop buying shoes for my children. We have that water problem everywhere. When taps run, the civil servants in that office find ways of stopping the flow, then extorting money from subscribers. They come around when everyone has gone to work and disconnect something so you will call when you return and part with money.'

'My children are already wearing shoes, so God help them. So you've come here to register to vote for poverty. Those who were poor often forget their poverty when they come to power. They are busy accumulating what they have found and do not want their fourth generation of children to go shoeless. Or perhaps you believe he will bring back the dead industries. Bata claims to be the most experienced shoe maker. It exited these lands. I was not surprised to see them strong and kicking in Asian countries, jobs for the youth. Maybe the oil- clogged waters will be cleaned so fish will breed and we will say goodbye to ice fish. My Mother Still refuses to touch 'dead fish' as she calls it'.

'O mine will make you feel like you are eating a corpse when she talks of ice fish and has made the children to hate it. Why is it taking these people so long to come with the election materials to start the registration? There has been no movement in the last hour.'

'I told you let's go and do something worthwhile but you insist the first day will not be bad. Now I've just talked to someone over there. He is number 11 and he came as early as 7am. They have condemned that list because someone used sheets of paper as the officials had not come. Now they have a notebook which the owner of this house behind us gave them and irrespective of the early comers he has started with the man, his family and friends.'

'Well, we are close by so it will get to us quick enough. It is important we register to vote. You know this is the first time a minority may break that jinx that it has to be wazobia or nothing.' Aboje almost nodded in agreement with the tall man but he looked the other way.

'So that's the issue? What of no winner, no vanquished. He is not a minority? You don't need to perform if you are a minority! You must stop selling that stupid idea,' said the bald head.

'Well, that is not really the main reason I must vote though that is also a plus. And who says he will not perform,' said the tall man with a sneer. He was showing some disgust.

'Well he is talking about "fresh air". He seems to have nothing to say other than fresh air which nature has endorsed us with in abundance. Or is he going to do what Malaysia has done? Provide air conditioners in all shops and houses and rent at cheap prices so our traders will stop running around and disgracing us?'

'That is possible, isn't it? Malaysia is only fifty years old, but see what it has achieved. Leaders in that country always want to leave something to be remembered for. One was supported by the owner of that Highland. A city on the mountain and when he won the election he built a dual road up that mountain and the skyways every tourist wants to hop on and fly above the rocks and streams and ravines to the biggest entertainment centre. And the other leader built the Twin Towers which Hollywood goes to shoot movies and tourists go at midnight to look at the waterworks. And another turned the night into day by planting high palms and hanging up millions of white, green, blue, red, and yellow bulbs. The towns come alive in the night and Malaysians have made sleep an unimportant part of their lives. I know it is possible because this country always calls on the minorities to repair damages done by wazobia and when it comes to the benefits. Wazobia! He will do it. Let's try him.'

'Listen to yourself! Can you do all these things you have listed in Malaysia without the technology that makes light a constant?' The bald head laughed sarcastically. Aboje thought that was very typical of Naija as his children would say.

'Let me tell you something, any creative leader can do all these in twelve months if he picks a right cabinet with creative people. Don't forget he cannot be in the PHCN and the other offices. It is for us all,' the tall man said, controlling his voice with an effort.

'Twelve months?' The bald head looked up at the tall man's face.

'Yes. Twelve months is plenty of time because he was there before and taking stock. Like a farmer taking stock from the last harvest you farmed/fished with others. What did you do and what did you not do. It is enough time to think back to when you hawked pure water, sold newspapers on dirty roads with open gutters or played drums like the winner of June 12, to pay fees and studied with lamps to pass exams and then moved into the hot seats of power. Twelve months is enough time to think of position and status and enough time to reflect on the absence of all the trappings and luxury which had come with power and status. Twelve months is enough time to think of this stupendous wealth you sit on and what you should do with it. It is enough time to reflect on what happens when this accumulated wealth cannot be enjoyed, when those who rush around you now will not be there, when your former assistants and advisers, when your former servants will look the other way when the

Botox-injected faces and tummy tucks and bleached faces and phony accents are all gone. Twelve months is enough time to do what the Tigers did because the foundations are already on ground. No one needs new researches, or resources or training. If it is copying, we can fall back on Aba 'original' manufacturers. He will get the universities equipped to copy all they have been researching and building on from other countries. Ah I am sure of his success,' the tall man concluded with a smile towards Aboje as if in some agreement. Aboje smiled in return but said nothing.

'You really mean this, don't you? This guy held same position of responsibility with large resources in how many years? Listen to yourself!' the bald man countered.

'The country has the manpower and money, only waiting for the man who will roll out the drums, stop sharing the spoils of money, lands, houses. In twelve months he can build the sidewalks and fill them with space for traders, tailors, food sellers, artisans without the ministry of works staff extorting them. Let the Aba traders make shoes instead of running around Asian towns to buy and come to re-sale. Let them stay home and marry their sweethearts instead of the humiliation they must take from Asian girls to avoid police harassment. They have become legalized foreign workers only allowed by law to work in the sub-sectors of mining/ quarrying, mangrove wood, stall/ cake/canteen/ catering, newspaper vendors, house and vehicles cleaner, car workshop workers (where they become spare parts dealers for home consumption) scrap metal cargo handling (where they are very soon accosted for stealing) welfare, home/spa/ hotel/golf caddy, whole sale and retail and textile (which they love and become "fashion dealers"). They work there because the Asians let them buy cheaply what they do not need. But legalized immigrants can only work for a maximum of two years. So they move from one country to the other and specialize in hiding from the police.'

'And I guess twelve months is enough time for Kaduna to do what Honda is doing in Bangkok, Thailand, with a capacity to assemble 240,000 cars a year!' came the bald man.

'And why not? We have the market!' The tall man almost shouted down his discussant's face.

'I think you are serious!' said the bald head, a little tired.

'Look, this is a new man. Life, someone said, is like a book. Every day has a new page, with adventure to tell, lesson to learn and tales about good deeds to remember. We have the past to remember and learn from. He will be wise to work closely with a man like the former military head of state who is challenging him. He is a man any wise and serious leader will do well to get close to. I think this one will,' the tall man said gently.

'He will get close to who? The man who will stop them from robbing the country dry? The man who will hunt them down to return the monies they looted? What's wrong with you?' The bald head was definitely angry now.

'You've suddenly lost your sense of reasoning. Please listen to the man making announcements,' said the tall man gently.

'He says we should return tomorrow. The machines have a problem of setting. We will return tomorrow Sunday. We will register and vote for his promise to stabilize electricity.'

Aboje turned and walked over to Ameh who had moved to the registration desk. He was talking in a subdued manner to a man with an INEC identification tag on his chest, a way he had with him when he was disappointed. Aboje only heard the last part of the man's response, 'Yes we will start with the list in this notebook tomorrow at 8am.' He tapped the notebook with his forefinger. The two men feeling diminished, drifted back to their homes without another word. The estate stretched before them, silent, the paraphernalia of plastics containing rubbish, bags containing all sorts of imaginable gabbage strewn around the containers, the contents of most scattered around by those who made their living from the rubbish heaps. Offensive smells oozed out of one with maggots spirallying from the bags into the gutter and the two men cupped their noses with their palms. Aboje had that strong conviction that he and many like him needed to vote. The promised fresh air seemed to waft round the umbrella and masqurade trees down the street waiting to be unleased, Aboje thought and suddenly he became oblivious of the foul stench from the rubbish heaps.

* * *

The next morning Aboje and Ameh walked down lessurely to the registration venue, grateful the rain had exhausted itself at about 4am. The weather was cool and much of yesterday's sulfurous emissions and the maggots had been washed away. It was a few minutes to 7am and the men wanted to be on line near the registration desk should anything happen to the list of names compiled the previous day. There were at least fifty men in two lines when they entered the school yard. They stepped in, Ameh on the other line and Aboje on the second, a little ahead and just then he heard the voice of the bald-headed man. Aboje looked at Ameh and both greeted the two men in front of them and asked how long the man in front of Ameh had been there. He said he had just come himself. Had gone to check the table but the INEC people had not come but he was sure they would not come late after the previous day. Ameh agreed with him and followed up the conversation with comments on the beautiful weather but Aboje's attention was with the man behind him talking to the tall man.

'You see how we wasted half of yesterday. I do hope the situation will be different today. I will register because of your pestering but I am not sure I want to vote for fresh air! Look its even cold this morning, very fresh, dirt washed away even though it's piled somewhere to some residents' annoyance.'

'O stop belittling important issues. That phrase is simply metaphorical. And I don't think the same situation will repeat itself. The operators of those machines are youth corpers who did not have the required training but it is nothing difficult. By the way, my heart is gladdened with the news that the book culture will be revived. That is part of the fresh air we are talking about.'

'People are talking about imagination, ideas, creativity which we see in Israel, desert country exporting to us apples and bananas. See their new capital city and attempt comparison. Even the old cities, have they stopped developing? See what the Brits did this Olympics when every one said no one would beat China. I bet Mexico will also spring surprises. Jos was and could house our hospitality but what is happening there? Some people are determined to make nonsense of it. And everyone just watches. This country has beautiful sights, waters, highlands. Lagos Island is standing dangerously on water. No one is doing anything about it. Let this creativity begin at the universities with the 26% of the national bugget. If people see our cities clean, they will want to come and see more. But see what is happening, if you have ideas and your superior has none, he chases you away, brings in someone more blunt than himself. He sees your creativity that will lead to innovations as a challenge to him. If this your book reading has anything to do with imagination and development, tell us so by doing something important, by beginning with, even if it is recycling. Five recycled water bottles can produce a shopping or school bag that can last for as long as the user is careful. But look behind you there. They burn the rubbish of useful things in the street, not to talk of the main disposing venue. They set fire to it. No recycling. If you do that those boys that go around picking things in the bin would be doing them with a purpose, not stealing from the houses they search dustbins.'

The man behind them with round eyeglasses cut in.

'I understand what you are saying. We went to a car factory in Bangkok to look at some Honda cars which had been damaged by floods and to be environmental friendly, the cars were to be destroyed to ensure that their parts would not be sold…!'

'A minus for Nigerian spare parts dealers,' a man in a green face cap said.

'These were cars submerged following Bangkok floods at an industrial estate. Many were evacuated but over a thousand cars were not lucky and the factory swore it would not close down. People must work with the government,' round specs added.

'If government is not too greedy or distrustful of creativity, if that happened here they will ask the company to close down,' green face concorded.

'Mmm?' the tall man seemed to grunt a question.

'Well if the company has no godfather...' started the bald head but the tall man cut in.

'People are more into buying cheap things from China Towns than to see in our towns things they can easily produce of better quality, because those with money prefer to go abroad and buy; from electronics to dresses and shoes. If they behaved like India, "what we don't make we don't need", it will be a step forward for the creative process which our president –to- be is advocating! He should start by stopping the importation of Kekenapep. Why in the whole wide world would anyone in his right senses allow the import of keke!'

'Now the registration officers are here. Young man, I hope you will start with those of us who wrote names yesterday,' shouted a pot bellied man third on Aboje's line. The young man nodded positively.

'I am number six on the line and this man here is five,' said the tall man to the registration officer who took the list down the line to tick the names of those in the notebook and move them up the line. Tall man and his bald friend moved ahead of Ameh and Aboje and very soon he was done.

'Young man, this is taking rather long but thank God I am through. Kene, I will see you in the evening. Right now I want to go queue up to buy fuel. There are rumours all money went into the election campaigns and subsidy is the only source,' the bald head said to his tall friend.

'Don't mind people, Bulus. It is the marketers. Whenever they want to make some money from black marketeering they talk of fuel subsidy to scare people and create a feeling of scarcity which drives people into buying at black market rates. But today is Sunday and I need to also get some fuel. I will join you there!' Kene said.

'Well I heard it is caused by diversion to neighbouring countries though I wonder why the people diverting are not arrested,' said a young woman with dreadlocks. She walked away to her car without waiting for a reply. Bulus looked after her for a while and turned to Kene,

'When you come, drive on until you find me and enter the queue in front of me!'

Aboje had also finished and was waiting for Ameh. He had fuel in his car but his wife's car was empty and he would pick the car to fill it up. He walked slowly towards the gate and stopped twice to greet a few aquaintances on the long queues, encouraging them to stay on and register. The sun was up and it was getting hot but most felt lucky that it was the heat rather than rain as most of the classrooms were locked and they would end up on the corridors with water splashing on them. Some of them looked tired but they would not give up, Aboje thought cheerfully. He walked away thoughtfully. His license had expired a week earlier and he had not noticed until the vehicle inspectors had stopped him on his way to work and asked for his papers. They had seized the car and only released it after he had paid a fine of twelve thousand naira. When he went to pick the car, it had been bashed leaving him with an untidy dent below the passenger front door. Nobody admitted seeing anyone do it. Two days later he went to their office to renew his license and got a fake. Tomorrow he would go there to make a complaint and wondered worriedly how long that would take him. He sghed loudly.

* * *

Aboje knew the petrol station manager who advised him to park on the other side of the road until they started serving. He promised that his boys would call him in through the out gate so it was a coincidence that Aboje was again parked behind Kene, talking across the road to his friend Bulus. He recognized Aboje and quickly called out.

'Ah there you are. There seem to be no movement. I parked over here where I can easily join the queue if cars start moving.' He waved to his friend.

'They claim they are offloading the fuel from the tanks to their pits. Someone told me they did that all evening yesterday and then closed and asked people to return today. Meanwhile they are selling to some selected cars at the extreme pump there and filling jerry cans to those boys who sell for a commission,' Bulus complained, getting out of his car.

'Well, it looks like this weekend will be spent on registration and fuel!' said Kene.

"I also need to service my second car. It consumes less fuel and it's the one I use during the week to and from my long distance office in Bwari,' Bulus said.

'Well you are not too far away and if they are honest with the sale to cars on queue, we should be out of here in the next hour. That woman over there looks sick,' Aboje said looking at a woman in a purple wrap round skirt and lose -fitted blouse leaning backwards on her Toyota Corrola.

'It is frustration. I moved away from her a short while ago, couldn`t bear her hissing and groaning and shuffling. A woman like that who can`t get a little black market and wait for a better day must have an unpleasant home front.'

'Lucky guys with wives like that are probably sleeping or hiding away somewhere only to appear when the woman has taken care of the problems.'

'Then what makes him a guy?'

'His friends don`t know that even the house he lives in the wife built it. He is the good guy around his friends, always eager to give a helping hand because he has no responsibility in his home.'

'The traditional long suffering wife!'

'Hey they`ve started selling!' Aboje called out to the two men engaged in their banter.

'Let me go and wait for the car in front of you to move before I join the line, then you will hear the barrage of curses from those behind you!' Kene said to Bulus.

As he joined the line in front of his friend, Aboje drove towards the out gate, the security man reconised him and pulled back the cross bar. Aboje drove in and spoke to the security man pointing a finger towards the woman. Aboje called to a younger man to go make way for the woman to pull out and drive in through the out gate. She drove in with a look of confusion and uncertainty, looking at faces that meant nothing to her. She did not recognize any of them. The boy pointed at Aboje and she prostrated in appreciation, tying and retying her scarf on her head. They served her first and she drove out, relief written all over her. She managed a smile too for the security man as she passed by the gate. Aboje drove out and headed for home. He needed a meal and a little sleep. He would go to the office later in the day to write some reports and arrange documents for the permanent secretary's hand over notes. He had been advised it would save him the rush and misunderstandings if he got things put together prior to his retirement. He was now due but things had been put on hold till after the elections. His colleagues were sure Aboje would 'take over the perm sec's chair.'

Kene pulled out of the station and waited for his friend whom he could see talking loudly to another man who was waiting his turn with much relief in his expressive hands and face. He drove out and stopped on the road next to Kene.

'Now you have a full tank; we wait for the subsidy removal,' Bulus laughed.

'I am going to the hospital right now to move my mother in-law to a private hospital!'

'Ah the strike is affecting the National Hospital too?'

'Yes, all government hospitals. These doctors are very insensitive. Rather than discussing with government it is strike, strike, strike. They end up with peanuts and a year later they are on it again.'

'I agree with the doctors. They work long, odd hours. Their salaries should be commensurate to their work schedules,' Bulus said with a passion.

'And so do others like the university teachers. You should see how much money goes out of this country to foreign universities. I am in the banking sector and can tell you. It is not funny. There are some countries whose embassies are here basically for that purpose. And in spite of the money they make from students they have no respect for them. They would invite the student for an interview, give him a two week visa and keep him for three months before giving him letter of admission and when the student goes for his student visa, he is charged huge sums for overstay. The students are frustrated but can't leave because they don't want to return to closed institutions. I hope the new government will see to the eradication of this menace!' said Kene who rarely made long speeches.

'The military caused this; they have never had any value for education but it does not mean the situation should continue. That is why democracy is here. My boys will return tonight,' Bulus said.

'By ABC bus?'

'No, with the last Air Nigeria which is about 8 pm. I have no liver for the pot holes and gullies on the road around which robbers target the buses. Okafo's daughter was raped last year on the Benin express way and she committed suicide. The family cannot live it.'

'So Nigeria Airways is operating?' said a man in a yellow shirt who had just finished urinating in the grass near a shopping plaza opposite the fuel station. The two men turned towards him and he continued, 'It used to be my favourite airline before it wound up shop. Well, even from the airport to the town now is no longer safe with the unending construction work. They could easily build that road at night with flood lights. That's what other countries are doing but the German and others here are just messing around, not even building good roads anymore.'

'Well, they know they can get away with anything with bribes. By the way, I said Air Nigeria, initially owned by a Briton but now sold to a Nigerian. He could not handle business in Nigeria. He says he will never come this way again. Do you see the traffic on Nyanya and Gwagwalada roads?' Bulus replied blandly with some irritation.

'They have made going in and out of the city a task I no longer wish to undertake. If you were here five years ago, you would not believe it is the same place. Try driving to Kado or Life Camp at 6pm. I guess that's the airline my cousin said someone in the queue at a bank said they were stranded in London and were asked to contribute money to buy fuel,'said yellow shirt.

'That is ridiculous. I don't think such a thing is possible. I am worried about the traffic on airport road. The check points do not help matters. It is police or soldiers or road safety. Each has something he is looking for and they make it look more like a bargain deal. And people just do not help matters with fake driving licenses, fake everything.' Bulus said slowly moving as a car honked behind him.

'Ah here are the police to supervise the sale of fuel. But they took long in coming,' Kene noted the mobile police men looking serious, shifting their guns from hand to shoulder.

'Yes I learnt they were all meeting in their DPO's offices to discuss the new legal checkpoint for the Tax fund. Many of them are not happy because at the end of the collection this time around, the money will go into a common purse,' Bulus pulled a little ahead to give way to the car, came out of his car and walked towards Kene and the yellow shirt talking.

'You can never check the many and different types and ways of collecting money from citizens. Right here at the petrol station, when they check "particulars" on the roads or search for missing cars which necessitates stopping all similar cars and asking for Christmas, Easter, Sallah or pure water. Forget, you and I will be the impoverished in spite of the official check point tax.'

'Transparency, I think this government can do it…' Kene looked at the man who had walked over and shook hands and introduced himself as 'Allex, owner of that Pharmacy.' He pointed.

'Man, I admire your confidence. Transparency is scarce commodity here my friend. If it were available our boys would not be on the streets hawking handkerchiefs and popcorn. The only way you become a millionaire in no time is to play politics. It's the only sure banker and you don't need to be smart, just be mean and less caring.' Allex smiled.

'Let me take this call… Yes Utang… A workshop? A good one with a big budget, that's good. I should do the papers for the presenters. How much? Six Hundred for four papers. Make it one million since I will write the papers for your presenters. No problem, a month is good time. Come to collect along with the money. Bye. My friend, that is a good by the way job,' Bulus said.

'Include me o,' Kene laughed getting into his car.

'I will ask some lecturer friends to write them for 50k each and in two weeks the work is done.'

'And you go away with 800. How long have you been doing that?' Kene asked.

'For two years now since I moved to Bwari. You know their condition. During that long strike without pay, the civil servants really used them. Initially they called them to write and present the papers at the seminars and gradually found that they could get their friends to present once the papers were done. Who listens anyway? It is just another convenient drain of budgeted funds.' Bulus laughed.

'Interesting. I must be at the hospital right away,' he said, waved to Allex and drove off.

Ameh took Cecilia to sign some claim papers at his friend's office. All those they met for one reason or the other were kind and helpful. Her husband was hard working and generous and that was the best they could do. It was unfortunate he took his replacement so hard. It was bad enough but this was the system and he should have learnt to live with it, they said. A few said the problem with him was that he refused to take what was available even when his boss gave him a free hand and his heart had weakened with contemplation. His secretary said as a Christian she believed he had done the right thing, what any honest God-fearing man would do and in her twenty two years none of her bosses had been more dedicated. She wished his spirit well. Having put all copies of the signed papers in her black bag, Cecilia followed Ameh down the stair case and out into the flairing sun. There were people and cars moving around but the streets and car park appeared hollow and lonely even as the offices up there had seemed empty and burdened. It was six months since the election and two months since Aboje's death.

THE LAKE SIDERS

ALTHOUGH THE LAKE STOOD THERE, securely fastened to the earth and, as always, the sun rose striking a deep red stretch across its unmoving surface, everyone around it was busy warming up, barely aware of its presence. These people who called themselves lake siders were nearby residents who jogged, walked or drove to the lakeside every morning for vigorous exercise or just a warm up or simply to socialize. The sun gently peeped out as they threw legs on the metal railings that kept them from falling over as they stretched their hands to touch their toes or bent their faces down to their knees with a count of ten or more. Some pushed up on the grass or concrete slabs, others walked or ran on the cobbled pathways on the field or the walkways by the waterside in pursuit of a healthy body and long life, as each believed. If you leaned on the railings you could see the fishes chasing in circles near the surface in tune with the crowd.

If you were early before 6am the moon looked down gracefully with that map of Africa on it, the street lights and security lights of houses in the distance sent their red, green and weak blue streaks across the lake proudly until the sun rose and dispelled them. The trees stood by the water at various angles, their leaves or shades reflecting on the water until the strong glow of the sun chased the shadows away leaving the leaves sadly still. At 6am the street lights went off as if in protest and in response some lake siders would run across the road to a nearby Chapel to say mass.

Many lake siders who went to work early, the bankers for instance, beat the sun to the water side Mondays to Fridays and as they ran or walked, watched it rise. At first its faint streaks reflected on the water and as hard as you looked at the sky you could not see it but it was right there on the water in several long lines. By the time you came round on your second run it had broken through the sky and struck the silent water with that huge fire ball and its arrogance that blinded the eye that looked at its face. Its strength seemed to weaken even the trees, the boats that had been moving smoothly with its occupants throwing nets into the water and even those who refused to notice its presence. No one failed to notice when the sun hit the water with that fiery ball. It penetrated your skin gently, then your eyes in a way that made it difficult for the eye to look at it as if demanding it to recognize its supremacy. And it made you feel the difference of the sweat of your labour at dawn and that which came by its presence. It made you take off the pull over and hang it on a tree or tie it round your waist but the freshness was only for a while. Some early comers like Ada and Chioma would smile and feel superior and often said to the sun, 'I beat you to it. You cannot choose to come out before your ordained time. The power God gave humans over you, powerful you may be.'

Then sometimes they would retort painfully, as if speaking for the sun, 'But you die, and I outlive you.' Every one with different advantages, Ada thought.

Ada was always satisfied when she got to the waterside before the sun and looked around for the fishermen returning in their boats with mild waves around them. She could not swim and often wondered what the depth was like. Sometimes she was tempted to find a long stick and test its depths but she never did. At other times she went close to a tree that had its stems or a sizeable part of it in the water but the slope made it uncomfortable. Others around may wonder what she was up to sliding down some steep slopes to the edge of the lake and suppose she slipped and no one was there or it was someone like her who could not swim? The life guards were sleeping soundly in the boats with the curtains drawn. She had passed by the boats many times and seen them fast asleep with a part of the curtain too short to shield them completely from prying eyes of joggers. Sometimes they woke up early and would be taking their bath from a bucket with water that had been fetched from the lake and it flowed back into the larger water rolling down on the grass.

Sometimes she saw a single man or a little group praying on a rock or under a tree in the field. They were far gone speaking in tongues to hear a cry in English if she slipped in an attempt to go near any of those trees as she was often tempted. Sometimes she would look enviously at the frogs and wish she understood their tongue as they hopped out of the water unto the grass, croaking. Then Ada would conclude that she would never know the depth of that water. Neither the fishes nor the frogs could answer her questions and the guards were often sleeping or taking their bath nearby but too naked for her to talk to them. And the fishermen were too far out on the lake.

On her early days she would have made two rounds of the walkway which covered less than half the lake before the sun shot its first shaft across the water. It often looked at first like a pillar down the water. Ada would stop and do a hundred skips and lean over the railings for a breath and watch the little fishes swimming around with little concern about the world above them. She was sure if her hand could reach them they would simply swim over it or would they nibble at it? A few times she saw long stretches across the water that disappeared in the distance and she was sure they were water snakes. Apart from the fishermen in their boats, she never saw anyone swim in that lake, the better if there were creepy things in there.

Now bright enough to remove fear of the dark spots around the mango and palm trees at the extreme end of the walk way, Ada would start her third lap with a slow jog skipping the single line of ants that rushed across in both directions. She felt sorry for them as some runner would soon disturb their peaceful, organized procession by stepping on them. The heaps of leaves which would also be run on even as she was going to do so right away was a response to the strong winds of the night but now a few flew down gently to join their compatriots waiting to be gathered with the plastics of drinks and burnt beside the water. The gentle fall of the leaves flowed along with the elderly men and women who made attempts at jogging but soon restrained themselves to walking in partnership with the leaves that flew gently across the walkways to the carpet grass and sometimes long enough into the lake. Often the leaves would drop on someone's head or shoulder and stayed there until another person who had stopped to rest and say 'hello' would pick it and drop it on the walkway. Sometimes the palm trees that extended their branches on the walkway were a danger to the eyes of new comers to the lake but it never took them long to know when and where to bend or move away.

The leaves sometimes fell on the horses tied with long ropes on to the palm trees beside the lake but they would often in search of their preferred grass cross the walkways, stretching the long ropes in the way of runners. Many of the runners and walkers skipped or hopped over it but the elderly women went close and lifted their legs gently hoping the horses would not raise their heads and by so doing heighten the spaces they needed to cross. It would be dangerous to have one of those ropes up between someone's legs, Ada winsed. Often the horses left their huge mounds of droppings on the walkway and you had to jump over it or move away from it. The horses were always foraging in the grass picking their choice but they always looked hungry, their seat bones prominent. One was often swinging his head to a large sore on his back to drive away flies that tormented him and one was going round and round in circles until the rope was wound round the palm tree to which it was tied. It appeared restless. Ada felt sorry she did not know much about horses to help it.

Sometimes the male horses would chase the females and people would hurry away from them or watch from a distance. A few dogs that accompanied their owners would step back and bark at the horses which paid them no attention at all apart from an occasional glance at a barking dog. A few male joggers would slow down near a horse that had its horsehood dangling down and Ada was often sure they were gossiping with some envy at the size they could not have. Once she had heard one say to his partner, 'That one is just standing and is bigger than me when I am in my full rough rider's mood!' His second looked back to see if they were alone but Ada was right behind them, then beside them and ahead of them, her head up, her eyes on the fruit of the palms ahead.

Then the sun would rise in all its glory, streaming down on the water, reflecting on the boats and canoes of the fishermen now tied with ropes to a stone or a nearby plant, draining away the coolness and drawing out sweat from the faces of both the runners and the walkers. Sometimes the sun's rays' reflection spread like a rainbow on the water and made you stop in stride for a little reflection on the power and beauty of nature. When this happened, the street and security lights which had earlier shone brightly on the water thinned and faded and by the time the rainbow reflections took over, the lights were completely out.

Ada was not only a beautiful woman. As a banker who was constantly in the eye of customers, she took her walk seriously. Years back, her main and favourite exercise was tennis but in the last ten years, since she moved to the new capital, there was no place for her to play tennis. She had found the IBB club but it was higher than her annual savings. She loved the place and had two friends and former school mates who were members. One was a high court judge and the other an INEC commissioner, both divorcees. She envied their freedom and successes which they said could never have come their way if they had not taken the difficult decision to walk. Ada loved their company and that of Generals both retired and serving and their elevated statuses but she would not ride on their backs and so she had had her last game one morning and had decided to register at a gym and in a year had shed the excess weight she had gained while searching for a tennis court. She had switched from tennis to squash and biking and walked on Saturdays until she moved into the estate by the lakeside. She no longer remembered the club she could not be a member.

The estate was large with beautiful roads and wide sidewalks. People described it as the largest estate in Africa and the best laidout in the country built by one of the former military presidents. Things like this were done only by the military since they had no national assembly and could use what could have been national assembly allowances to do some projects such as this. Ada loved the peace of the estate, its good roads and sidewalks where she walked and jogged for an hour every morning. She made many friends walking the roads, crescents and avenues but her most constant companions were Florence and Fr. Solomon. Florence also worked in a bank so they had a lot to talk about. Fr. Solomon was not only a priest in one of the parishes she frequented but also loved pets and she promised him a cat while he promised her a dog. They eventually redeemed their pledges over a lunch in his house and a dinner in hers.

Whenever Ada did not want to meet any of these regular friends, she took some other routes, short, well groomed with palms, whispering vines and high hedges of masquerade plants and a variety of other plants. On many of the gates, notices asked people to stay away as there were dangerous dogs. Some gates simply pasted a picture of a dog or two. A few dogs barked from some gates as Ada walked by but she was not afraid of dogs. She had kept and bred many dogs. Ada enjoyed reading the messages on gates or walls and there was always something new like a new nursery or primary school all of which were always 'International', or a clinic/maternity, dental, eye hospital. Once in a while a new water or beverages depot sign appeared on the wall of a fence or gate. Out of her three directions was a mosque and she would encounter people rushing in one direction as she went and returned. Sometimes they would look at the rosary in her hand and hold back their greetings so as not to interrupt her prayer. The rosary reduced the distance.

Ada wondered why she had not seen that sight for almost six months of walking the well-groomed side of the estate. 'Beware of dangerous snakes. Trespassers will be swallowed.' Where were the snakes kept in the compound, Ada wondered. Did they know their owners and frequent visitors like dogs? Ada hated snakes no matter the beauty of their colours. She had killed a few snakes around the house during the rainy seasons but the anxiety remained days after. Once she had driven over a huge snake as it crossed a path near a farmland not far from a scool she was visiting. She had remained in the car with the screens wound up and watched the snake dive several times in its full height of over ten feet before lying still. Then the security men had picked it on a long pole and taken it away. They said it was good meat. For the rest of the day Ada could not take her mind off the snake as it sumasaulted above the high grasses while she watched, open-mouthed. That snake could certainly swallow a big man.

Ada looked at the red and green prints of the 'swallow' and wondered if it had any thing to do with the colour of the snakes. With a frown she turned to face her direction and saw the car again stop a short distance ahead of her and two men step out walking towards her. She remembered from the triple even number that she had seen the car when she turned out of her close to join the main road. Then she had seen it again near the mosque and thought the occupants were going for prayer. She slowed and crossed the road to the next gate where she could see a dog through the slants and hit the gate with a fist. The dog barked, others responded and someone asked 'Who is there?' The men hurriedly returned to the car and drove off as some gates began to open. Ada knew the dogs were not just positively extraneous but useful to community of passersby.

She quickly walked home with this foreboding in spite of some guards coming out with water in kettles for ablution and the knowledge that she was out of danger. Were the men kidnappers? Did they know her? Had they been monitoring her and knew she came out every morning and had waited for her. What did they want from her? She was not rich or she would have joined the IBB club. If they were kidnappers what did they think they would get from her family? They were not rich people. Were they hired assassins? She was not even a branch manager to have refused some bitter person a loan or gotten into some deal. She was not involved in many love affairs and the few… both parties simply drifted away, no quarrels, no fights, no expectations. Perhaps they were ritualists and were after any eyes or heart or breasts. She shuddered.

Ada did not walk the estate again. She chose the lakeside and drove there at first at 6am and later found people were there much earlier and so drove there at 5.40 when the street lights set the lake aglow. But she would not go near the water at the far end where bushes grew tall until 6.15 when daylight splashed the cobbled run ways and the ever green trees and grasses as well as the field where boys changed into their different colours of pants and tops to play football.

The lakesiders had striking differences if you paid a little attention. They were not there just to run or walk or play football or gist. On her second day on the walk/run way Ada met an elderly lady in white shorts, pink T-shirt and yellow socks in white canvas shoes. She greeted jovially and pulled out her hand from the pocket of the shorts for a handshake. She told Ada it was good to see that people were getting conscious of the usefulness of a good exercise. She said she had recently retired from Customs and Excise and drove every morning from Wuse to the lakeside and it was quite fulfilling. She waved with a smile to a man who ran past and then turned to Ada, 'You see this man, he is active but I have told him many times he needs to watch his diet. He will do this stretch ten times and then replace it with a huge breakfast of white bread and eggs with a mug of coffee. He says he doesn't take lunch but would end the day with a mound of pounded yam, Eba or Akpu with a bowl of palm kernel soup and all the varieties of meat. And wash it down with some bottles of beer. Now he says it is red wine.

'You must join us at the monthly Gracefully Aging fellowship. You will love the diet talks and no matter how much you think of your exposure and experience, you will grasp something new. Some doctors come to give talks on nutrition once in a month and that day is today. For example I am now having just vegetable juice for breakfast and it is soooo refreshing! What's your name?'

'Ada'

'Well, Ada I am Rosemary Inne and don't miss that GRAF meeting. It is 5 pm.'

Through Rosemary Inne Ada joined a group of men and women who did some aerobic exercises every Saturday morning at an announced and fixed time of 7 a.m. Ada would come at 6 and run two rounds of the walk way and then begin to walk and chat with some early comers but the team would sometimes be assembled at 8.30 and in the process of waiting, she found another group run by an active and charming young man who would lift you on his back, lay you down on a mat and give you a few minutes of wonderful massage to ragae and hip-hop sounds blaring from musical instruments run by a gen set under a tree. He was good company for those with frustrated and dead- end jobs and the kind of bosses trying unsuccessfully to be in control. He would say, 'This is good for those in offices where gossip is the mainstay.' And it would remind Ada of Chidinma who believed in gossip as a means to her career growth. She made it a duty to prostrate and bow to her superiors until she gained their confidence and then she would begin to suggest their love for the next senior colleague until the conversationlist contradicted what she had implied. Then she would go to the next person and before long she was in and out of offices telling the other what this person had said; then pleading for protection in her next promotion as the other had said this same person told someone she would not be promoted. By so doing she got every body trying to protect her and when any got her gist and confronted her she would say she was misunderstood. She was in the habit of telling her non banker friends and family she was almost there and very soon she would show her so called superiors who she really was.

It was from this small great guy Adamu that Ada first heard an analysis of lakesiders. The first were men who came in search of girls. He called them Casanovas. Then there were the senior girls with good jobs who came to find men to marry, and there were the young men who came to look for older women with a good purse and the girls who wanted someone to pay for their shopping or pay their rents. He talked to another young man who was putting laces on his shoes preparatory to a football practice while he fixed the wires on his speakers and the deck. The shoe lacer said he had forgotten those who just came to talk or watch. They both looked at a lone figure on a slab in the distance. Ada was stepping close by on some steps and listened to their chat with little interest as she counted to a hundred steps then ran off for her third round.

It was Ada's third week and she was beginning to feel at home with other lakesiders. She recognized several early risers whom she came before or met. This morning it was Mr. Ayodele as she had heard a few lakesiders address him. Yesterday he had greeted Ada in a most friendly tone and asked her to join him but after the second stretch, she could not keep his pace and took a diversion with another jogger. Today he offered to help her do some pushups. He said it was good to help keep her flanks as smooth as they were. He took her hand and led her to a corner enclosed by a large rock and two big trees, the planner's designs that captured the extensions into the lake with built concrete slides surrounded by trees. Ada had seen people going in to those extensions but had never diverted into them. They served as resting places. Mr. Ayodele pulled her down and stretched her legs down a concrete slab and squatted on them holding her by the knees.

'Now you rise and touch my shoulders,' he said.

Ada did it 20 times and stopped, breathing hard.

'Don't be lazy. You are going fifty times.'

Ada did another ten and stopped. Ayodele pulled her up into a sitting position and sat next to her, his hand round her waist pulling her against him.

'What's your name?'

'Ada.'

'You work?

'Silver Bank.'

'I work at Energy house. Can we have lunch today?'

'Not today. I have a meeting that will run late.'

'Tomorrow?'

'I will let you know if I can.'

'You must,' and he made attempts at a kiss. Ada stood up and ran to the open stretch, walking without stopping till she got to Adamu and his registered members. She joined the group next to Chioma whom they had met at the diet fellowship and they had taken to each other. They said 'hi' and continued with the warm ups.

As they took deep breaths before the next session, Chioma drew up to Ada, 'I saw you with Mr. Ayodele. What was he saying to you?'

'Inviting me to lunch.'

'He is good at that. He tried it with me. I got him to do some expensive shopping for me. There is hardly any woman here he has not tried to toast.'

'I told him I was busy today and not sure of tomorrow.'

'Good for him.'

It was 7 and time to leave. The next day Ayodele was jogging with another light-skinned thirtish woman and Ada was with Chioma. They were in opposite directions. Chioma shouted her greetings and he responded with a smile to her and a wave to Ada. Nobody stopped. They had some twenty minutes to go, and the sun was announcing its rise as it shot a fire glow across the water. Ada smiled with the thought, 'I beat you to it.'

'Good morning,' came a husky voice. Ada turned around and her eyes met a wide grin and an outstretched hand.

'Good morning,' she shook the hand, strong, hairy, wet palm. She hated wet palms.

'I am engineer Uko.'

'Ada'. She started stepping, using the nearest curb.

'That's too low. Come up here,' said engineer Uko, cheerily taking her hand.

'No, that's a little too high for me,' Ada cut him off, taking away her hand. He waited, counting out loud. She stopped at a hundred and started running. He followed.

'You live near here?'

'Yes.'

'Your office?'

'Silver Bank'.

'Can we have dinner, talk? I have been admiring you in the last one week and really want to know you better.'

'No chance.'

'What of Saturday, lunch?'

'I usually have my lunch at the gym where I walk out.'

'They have a restaurant?'

'Good food. Low fat, calorie free and delicious food. Fruit drinks made on request.'

'Will call you.'

'Good bye.'

He turned and ran off.

A heavy man jogged past, lifting his thumb to her in greeting. He was breathing hard. Ada waved back with a smile. She looked at the backsides of the three women before talking loudly in one of the many languages. One swished, the middle one wriggled, the other wobbled so disjointedly Ada looked ahead and picked speed, ran past them and joined a girl of about twenty four who complained to no one in particular, 'Why am I so tired this morning? O dear am fagged and I've not done half a kilo. Damm!'

Ada ran past her looking out for the young man who slept in a small building, obviously a toilet which was not used and remained locked. He had broken a lower part of the door where he made his entrance. In the morning he walked along with others paying particular attention to women. The previous day some guys had beaten him mercilessly for touching a woman's breast. Ada could not understand why they beat the poor guy so badly. It was obvious he needed to be in a psychiatric hospital. The signs were all there even though he was still clean and could at times be seen brushing his teeth in a corner from a bottle of water.

It was Saturday late morning and Ada had ordered her food and was reading a Blueprint editorial when engineer Uko walked in with his wide grin trademark. He was in a pair of jeans and pink striped shirt which suited his 6 feet slim trunk. The chef walked over with the menu.

'I will take whatever she is taking,' he said. The chef was happy. He went off and, shortly, the chicken corn soup was served. He looked at it quizzically and wondered aloud, 'Will I be able to eat this?'

'Then make your order. You may not like the shrimp dish either,' Ada said with a frown.

'You like it. I will learn to like it.' He ate tenderly at first and then gobbled it with great enyoyment.

'Though I prefer our local food, this is not bad.' He watched Ada for a while and then said, 'You have beautiful hands, an artist delight'. Ada had heard that before. Too many times it had long stopped giving her the thrills. She went on with her starter.

'How long have you been in the city?'

'Over ten years,' she said

'I came here not long ago, after the Jos crises. I lost my wife there. She was pregnant with her first child. I almost killed myself. My in-laws saved me from myself. It is three years now but it's been difficult. Since then you are the first woman who has stirred anything in me,' he smiled almost sadly.

'Well I am sure your late wife will want you to live,' Ada said, gently wiping her lips and pushing the bowl away. The young man collected the dishes.

'That's what everybody has been telling me but they don't understand. My wife and I were very close. We even had a common account. She was a friend, a sister. She was four years older than me but it didn't take long before those who were initially questioning me picking an older girl began to appreciate her?'

'How old are you?

'Thirty-two, and you?'

'I don't discuss my age.'

'But if we became…. You know I don't do friendship. I go straight to the point. What if I asked you to marry me? You can't keep your age from me. I mean it. I am not in this for friendship.'

'Mmm.'

The food came. Engineer Uko finished his and half of Ada's.

'I don't like to waste food,' he said.

Then they finished their drinks and the discussions were getting rather too personal and Ada asked if they could move to the pool.

'Yes', he said, getting up. Ada asked for the bill and as they waited Engineer Uko moved to admire some paintings on the wall. Ada settled the bill and as they moved out, Engineer Uko asked,'How much did you pay?'

'Thirteen.'

'I owe you.'

Ada said nothing. They moved over to the pool and on the side, two men played table tennis. Engineer Uko walked over to them and greeted cheerfully, shaking hands. One of them asked if he played.

'I was a champion', he said. The man said he was tired and needed a drink. His partner just came. He had played two men. Engineer Uko collected the batten; he admired its quality but said it was light. He bounced the ball twice and then shot. The second player returned the ball with a swift shot and Engineer Uko missed it. He blamed it on the food he had eaten, adjusted his trousers and looked at Ada with a conspiratory grin.

Ada chatted with the man whose drink had come and he was drinking with relish. It was water melon juice. He asked Ada if she wanted a drink. She had just had lunch, she told him. When Ada saw he was well rested, relaxed and looking contentedly at his empty cup of juice, she picked her bag. Engineer Uko finished the game and promised them they would meet again and hurried after Ada.

'Which way are you going?' he asked Ada.

'Appo.'

'I don't have my car with me and I am going to Finance Quarters.'

'I will drop you off some where.'

'Thanks and I owe you.'

'Yeah.'

Monday morning Ada got a call repeatedly from the same number. She was at a meeting and she did not know this number. On her way home she remembered the call and checked the number, 7 calls. She dialed.

'Hello, this is Engineer Uko. I want to see you. It's urgent.'

'I am on my way to Amigo.'

'Can I meet you there?'

'Ok.'

Half hour later, Ada drove into Amigo. Engineer Uko was by the gate.

'Hi.'

'Hi.' They went around, Ada picking things into a basket Engineer Uko carried.

'There is a job I am doing at Karu. It's a big job but the owner travelled for the hajj. I need some money. I will pay back as soon as the man returns.'

'How much?'

'I just need what to pay the workers. Three hundred. You know what it means with daily paid workers. They could linch one.'

'I am sorry I don't have that money.'

'Well, anything you can part with. It is very urgent. Whatever you can give to me. I will see what to do.'

'I am sorry I can't give you any money.' Ada collected the basket, went to the cashier, paid and collected her shopping. Engineer Uko came after her. He had lost his grin. He was pleading. One of the folded edges of his jeans had dropped. It was threaded. His sandals had a broken strap. Ada got into her car but did not open the passenger door. She waved to him and drove off.

Two weeks later Ada met one of the lakesiders she had not seen for a while.

'Did you travel?' Ada asked.

'No, I have joined the Philip Uko group. I need to work on my stomach. Adamu is good but focuses on aerobics. Philip is good at push ups.'

'Where is your group?'

'On the other side of the lake,' she pointed to an isolated patch behind a rock.

'We come at 5 and by 6 when most people come, we are on our way.'

'Great. Have a lovely day.'

'You too. And by the way we now pay a thousand a month to keep this place clean since government or whoever they privaticed it to does not care how the place is kept. You can see the the disposable containers around. We bought them. Mr. Obiano is the chair.'

Ada slowed down to listen to two men arguing over rights to the gate houses where they slept. One said in a deep polished voice. 'You don't even appreciate the matt I gave you. Was I not the one who showed you that room?'

'I am not talking about that and I…'

Ada moved on wondering why their families would not take them to a psychiatrist before they started taking off their clothes and chasing people around the lake. They were not in very bad shape yet but one was growing a bushy beard. He was clean shaven some weeks back with good shoes and a clean shirt. Now he was looking rough, more like, not well. Members of Lakeside had offered him a job to pick the bags and water bottles picknikers threw around the walkways but he had refused. He said he was a university student and that kind of job was below him for whatever fee. Ada sighed, looking towards the sun splashed water and decided she was done for the day.

THE CABALS

'I NEED TO IRON THESE things tonight,' Mom said looking at the gen set that would not start. We had not had electricity in my aunt's house in Kado Estate Abuja in the last two days since our arrival. Light was from the gen. This evening we found the place in darkness on getting to the house from places we had visited all day. She had wanted to send some dresses to the dry cleaner the previous day as she usually travelled light but my aunt had insisted her dresses could be washed that morning and ironed at night when the gen came on. Last night my mother and aunt had sat before the TV for hours listening to discussions on the so many committees set up to probe contracts or budgets. They were particularly interested in news about committees to investigate an estimated N200 billion allegedly missing pension fund and another to look into electricity supply but as much as the members talked it was not certain when the lights would stabilize.

My aunt's neighbours, Mr. and Mrs. Odife, had come in to listen to the news as their inverter had died off without electricity to charge it for two consecutive days. Last night they had left after the news sure the light would be restored before daybreak but that did not happen and their inverter could not be charged and so this evening they had to come again to listen to news in my aunt's house and also kill time. My mother was rather nihilistic about any progress in these matters and hardly said anything. Mr. Odife was optimistic especially when the committee on electricity supply went to the National Assembly with its report. He kept repeating that it was only a matter of time and from the way my mother looked at him I knew what she would say and I was glad she said nothing. Once in a while when such issuess came up, she would say, 'When they tell you when it will happen and I see it happening I will believe.' A Thomas one may say, but that was my mother. What shocked everyone that evening was the news that the committee on the sale of houses had concluded that it was not the management that appropriated the money from the sale of the Federal Houses but a cabal! Who was this cabal, my aunt had asked with her hands raised high up and her mouth wide open. My mother had looked unperturbed.

My mother was a traveler for as long as I could remember and sometimes we traveled with her even on foreign trips where we had relations or friends where she would leave us for a few days. While she was busy at some conference or workshop, we would do some sight seeing, visit a reading room, a park, go to a cinema and do some window shopping. Travels were always a joy because all we looked forward to was boarding the aircraft and being treated special. As kids we got toys and lots of sweets and picture books. Sometimes we got something really special especially on KLM. My mom had long concluded that government was the place where cabals were groomed, from clerks to directors. 'Watch the eyes of the messenger who took your file to the next room and the clerk who had told you for days the file could not be found till you understood his body language, my mother would say. Then the man who would take the file to the director would surely demand half your annual earnings if you were trying to get a house allocation and the director who recommended a house for the minister's approval? You would need to go to your bank to take a loan.' She said she had seen it all and simply laughed when the committee cried out about the cabal in the sale of houses. Every one of them was a cabal, she said.

At the airports I would notice my mom smile a lot at the customs and immigration officers who always had something to say to her. But my mom always had a smile for everyone. Sometimes she would give a few notes from her bag and the officials would grab it quickly and put it away in a hurry but I had always known my mom for her generosity. The only significant difference is that these people at the airport were not as expressive in their appreciation as others my mother tipped or 'dashed'. Sometimes my mom would complain loudly, 'I may as well take the first class if I have to pay this much for an economy ticket.' This was when she was told at the check-in counter that the aircraft was full and then someone went behind the counter to get her a ticket in her name with a seat number at an exorbitant cost.

Whenever my Mom was told the plane was full she would simply step back and pull her bag after her. At this point someone who was standing there all the while listening to the conversation between her and the airline staff across the counter would step to her and ask her to bring the money for him to get her a ticket. Then he would take her to a seat away from the counter, walk away and find his way behind the counter and after a long while, when he heard the last boarding call, would rush to her and declare that a seat was available but at so so cost. If mom had an appointment to beat, she would negotiate and eventually pay a sum and then the guy would collect her ID card and disappear again and reappear with a ticket all in her name and it would be legal. She would hurry and board the plane and discover to her amazement that there were lots of seats and the plane would often take another thirty minutes or more to take off.

The first time I travelled alone was with a group of students on a leadership training to Madison, U.S.A. We had an escort from the embassy who did all the buying of tickets and checking-in as my mother used to but the escort did not dash. The airport customs and immigration people appeared serious when they saw the white man holding air tickets and quickly passed us on. They were really polite, more polite to us than to other travelers. They were especially serious and careful with whites who wore face caps and jackets with large pockets and those who strapped to their waists some electronic gadgets.

The airport workers were not a part of our discussion as we went round New York and then Madison but the airports were a focus, especially the first time travelers among us. We compared the space at the foreign airports and ours wondering if it was lack of money or because we did not have as many travelers. But it could not be money. Everyone said we had it when they heard we were Nigerians. We also compared the many checks in Lagos even though at that time our hand luggages were checked only twice. We talked about the delays, the capacity and the unique attitudes of our airport staff, very unique indeed.

In 2011 I travelled alone for the first time. It began at the embassy where my mom had to pay N10, 000 for a one thousand naira visa. The woman there never came short of reasons why money had to be paid for something. She always said she was helping. She even expected my mom to be grateful because if she were travelling for business she would pay more. When mom narrated the story later to a family friend, he said it was the system even with the acadas who ought to make the difference. He had expressed disgust at a deputy vice chancellor who came out of his house in a tattered looking singlet to give him an admission letter for which he had paid one hundred and fifty thousand naira.

As he told my mom this incident he shook his head and said he would never forget the man coming out to meet him in a discoloured singlet with holes in it. I remembered the story each time my mom sent me to water board or any other government parastatal with an envelope which I knew contained money. She hated it but knew that things would never be done. She said if she did not co-oporate and complained to anyone you could as well say good bye to whatever you hoped for. It happened once when she took a tenant to the police. The tenant gave someone money and mom was detained on a bench for disturbance of peace till the next morning when a friend commissioner of police showed up. Only then was the tenant escorted to remove his belongings from the house.

As we left the visa office that day I felt sorry I had put my mom through this. It all started with my university which failed to get an accreditation for my program four years after we had started and I could not get a transfer to another Nigerian university of Technology because I had to remedy chemistry in which I had a p8 at SSCE. My mom had asked me to write the subject again while doing the remedial programme but I had ignored the advice and was paying dearly now. Other universities refused to give me a transfer unless the remedial was theirs. Sadly my mother had to look to this country for a resolution to finishing my course. She never liked the idea of us going out for a first degree in the first place. She said we would find things difficult if we had a first degree outside. She said we would be better off if we had a university education that inculcated in us our cultural heritage and other peculiarities. How could we deal with cabals and dash and egunje at every turn if we were not familiar with them?

I had two weeks for my interview and we all thought we had time until we went to the embassy. The woman said they would not accept an invitation from the internet. We should ask the school to send a proper letter on their letter-headed paper. There was a problem here because, earlier, our application on the Nipost fast mail took almost three weeks. We had tracked it online. We didn't have that much time so we asked a friend there to scan the letter and email it. At first the woman refused to accept the scan but the envelope Mom gave me did the trick.

Meanwhile my passport needed renewing and I spent days waiting in a canopy where sometimes rain beat us mercilessly. Twice I left with the immigration staff because they told me to wait and I had to hire a taxi to get home at 10pm. The reason we were given was that senators' passports were being processed. I spent the day watching certain people come in and 'talk' to those whose job seem to be to receive these people and then they would be led in and shortly after they would come out and leave us sitting and waiting. The following day they would again walk in casually, ask for the person they had spoken to the previous day and he would be called in and escorted out, his passport in hand. If we the waiters went to them they would ask when we submitted and then ask us to wait or come back the next day and not until my mother returned from a trip and went to see her old school mates did I get the document which I had virtually given up.

But not until I arrived Lagos did the worst of the cabals confront me. We the students were virtually marked. One guy I had got aquainted with while waiting to check-in was sent away for non clearance by the drugs unit. No one had told us of this clearance till now. I was asked how much I had and I told them showing them my school fees, feeding, accommodation and bus fares my mother had carefully calculated for a month until I opened an account for her to send me money. They took 200 USD and handed the rest back and I got the clearance. I held back my tears because I hated to call Mom to say the money she carefully calculated for my upkeep had been reduced by one week in accommodation and bus fare. Or that I may now have a meal a day until she sent some more money.

The checkpoints too had tripled and all the naira notes I had taken for when I would return were cleaned out. They asked or begged the men and women but just took from us guys even with threats. And the mean looking ones were strategically located. They barked at us and put the fear of

Satan in us. You just knew that they were never short of reasons to nail you and keep you from catching your flight. They knew you just wanted to get on that plane so you could get to school on time. They did not care whether you got on that plane or not and they did not want you to cheat others so you had to pay or return home. You could not play tough because they were the law and you would be the loser. I now understood why Ralph was determined to join the police after graduation. He said he could not change the system. No one wanted it changed but he would be the law. People would fear him because he would do anthing, even kill and get away with it. As I thought about my loss at the airport I toyed with Ralph's idea for a while, knowing Mom would not even consider it.

One of the boys Ademola did not have a yellow card. They waved him to someone who took him to a corner, gave him a signed and stamped yellow card for N2,500. He ran back afraid that his journey would end there. He now had a card he hugged delicately without the vaccination. I asked to see it. He gave it carefully like a diamond watching to be sure I treated it right. I opened the pages and compared it with mine. It was the same with the signature and stamps in the right places except this one was Lagos state. How did they get the stamps and signature the same as those of us who had been vaccinated? It had the same number and a stamp that bore the approved vaccination center, Federal Republic of Nija. I returned it to Ademola, my airport difficulties partner. Pius and I had checked-in our baggage but we had waited for him, sorry for him but glad for him too that he had resolved one problem.

At the Departure Gate, the two men just asked what we had for them. Ademola turned to me, 'Demi, do you have N200?' I gave him. He gave them. Pius gave them. I gave them last. They waved us on. It was at the next point I paid my last N500. We were stepping out with relief when the NDLEA accosted us. It was here my 200 USD was taken. It was here Ademola was turned back. He did not have money. His father had asked him to go and he'd pay money into his account. All he had on him was 20 USD and the money he had spent on the yellow card. He cried, we wept in our hearts with him but we could not help him. He was asked to go get a clearance.

When my mother scolded me for showing them my money, she did not know that I might have returned to Kano if I had not paid and would have had to start all over again. It could have cost us more. They were the law. I arrived my destination with much relief which was short-lived. My three month visa was cancelled and a two week one stamped in my passport. I did not worry. My interview was that morning. I was tired but proficiency test in English I could handle in Cambridge. This was a post-colonial colony like my own country and in any case I spoke no other language but English, nothing to be proud of but there I was, a child of two parents who had different tongues and spoke English to each other and to us. When I got to the venue of the interview the two men and a woman took one look at me and asked me to go and rest and come back Monday as this was a Friday. I went to a hotel and called home.

That Monday I did my interview and was told to go and wait for the outcome which would be in about a week. But it was not until September, three months after that I got a letter of admission by which time I needed to pay for an overstay. My mother was flabbergasted. I now knew why my three month visa was cut to two weeks.

My second trip was horrendous. The cabals had a reason and were vicious. It was Christmas, they kept repeating. I stayed behind a woman whom some guys, I was not sure if they were staff, promised to assist check-in fast without hazzle. They did and she gave them N1000 in appreciation but was still discussing with people who had come to see her off when I joined her at the box and bag search before check-in.

'How Christmas, madam,' the official asked.

'Fine, thank you,' madam replied.

'What do you have in here?'

'Personal things.'

'Merry Christmas,' said a second.

'Merry Christmas.'

'Any Christmas for the boys?' The woman gave them N1000 and passed on. I gave N500 and passed on. We were at the good bye point. A guy rushed to me with a brown paper bag.

'Please help me give this to my sister. It is popcorn.'

'Popcorn!' I looked at him.

'Call her to come and collect it. Why didn't you give her before now?' The security man at the good bye gate said and turned to madam.

'They refused her coming out,' the guy said desperately.

'Any Christmas for us,' the officer said, smiling at madam and ignoring the guy with the popcorn. She gave them N1000. I gave them N200.

'Please,' the guy with the popcorn said again looking at me.

'Sorry I can't take your popcorn,' I said to him, keeping close behind the madam.

'Don't mind him,' said the woman! Popcorn indeed!'

We walked the red and green and black tapes to the exit stamp counter. The passport was stamped and passed on to the two women ahead of us before the scanner. We passed the scanner and collected our shoes on the belt.

'Open your bag,' one of them said, still holding the passport

'No need,' the second said, 'but do us Christmas!' The madam gave N1000. They complained. She added another N1000. I gave N500. We moved to the NDLEA. They hardly looked at me. All I carried was my laptop.

'Where to, madam?'

'Singapore.'

'Do you have the clearance?' He looked at her passport.

'What is that,' asked the woman, showing some annoyance for the first time. She seemed to have had enough. I picked the bowl containing her shoes and wrist watch and handed it to her. She collected her shoes, put them on and then the wrist watch.

'What do you mean clearance? Clearance from what?'

'Is that your son?' she looked at me.

'Yes, what is the problem? Where and for what are we being cleared?'

'At the Head office but seeing that you are a woman of integrity, I don't expect you to be involved in drugs. But your route is a busy one for drugs and that's why…'

'But we should have been informed before we got here, not at the check-in point,' the woman cut him mid way.

'You know someone in your position with a son schooling abroad should know what's going on.'

'You know for a woman who has a child schooling out there you ought to know the issues so you can also advice him,' said the second

'Any problem?' another uniformed officer walked to them.

'No. Please give this professor and her son the clearance. Please go with him,' he said to the madam whom from her papers they knew she was a professor.

'The woman moved over and I appreciatively followed. He took a while, showed us a paper, a copy of someone's clearance. The woman looked briefly without reading what was on it and dropped it beside his computer and looked the other way. The man looked at his colleague who nodded. He picked two pieces of paper cut in small squares with a signature. He wrote the date and time and handed it to the woman who collected them without giving neither him nor the paper a look and handed one to me as we walked away towards the waiting hall.

This was a Christmas gift indeed. I thanked the woman after we had passed them. For young guys like me, this was always the most trying point at the airport. This was where I had lost $200 and Ademola had missed his flight. This was the point students dreaded. This was the point you were detained for no reason other than wearing an afro haircut or Mohawk. Louis was detained for eight hours, given food and made to go to the toilet several times, then released. He missed his flight and an interview. I had saved

$200 from gifts family friends had given me for Christmas for this purpose. I could not tell my mother. I was sure she would not understand. The professor had saved me money, harassment and intimidations from one set of cabals this time around. It was not often you met a professor who gave you one look and adopted you as a son at a most crucial time. They had missed out something important which could have earned them money that Christmas. The professor was not even travelling to the same country as I was. We parted ways in Dubai.

This year I chose to come home after the New Year. It was not really a choice as I could not get a flight before the 9th of January. I however could have changed flights but I preferred the airline I had booked and of course I wouldn't be returning at Christmas. I couldn't tell what returning at Christmas would be like at the airport. Then two days before my return my sister called. The labour strike would begin the day of my arrival. She wanted me to find out if my trip would be possible. I was not worried because I had a long holiday which was why I didn't bother with the rush period of Christmas. I was also sure the strike would not go beyond three days and it wouldn't do much to my holiday. I checked anyway. The strike did not affect international flights so on that 9th I flew home and arrived Lagos on the 10th. I had little luggage which consisted of my bag which I checked-in and a laptop for hand baggage.

As I made for the way out the NDLEA asked me to step aside. I did. They asked me to open my bag. I did. They searched and found nothing. They took me to another office and searched my body and scanned me. They sent me to another room with three other guys sitting on a bench. They asked me to sit there. I sat there. They brought me a bottle of water and meat pie. They said I should eat and drink all the water. I had a good meal on the plane and wasn't hungry and it had been long I stopped eating pies. But I wanted to get home and did not argue. My mom had booked me a flight for 5 p. m. It was now 2.20 p. m. I ate the meat pie and drank the water while a woman watched me. I dozed off and when I opened my eyes it was 4.06. I was left with a guy. I wondered what had happened to the other two. A man with flared nose walked over and faced me.

'Where are you going?'

'Kano.' I showed him my ticket. He looked at it and asked if I was a trader. I told him I was a student coming home on holiday.

He said there were no local flights and where was I going to stay in Lagos. I told him I had a sister in Lagos and she or her husband would pick me if I couldn't leave.

'Where do they work?'

'My sister works in a bank and her husband runs a private company.'

'Well, be careful of bad company,' he said as if he caught me in company. I said nothing.

'You can go.'

I picked my bag in one hand and hung my laptop bag on my shoulder and walked out slowly. I was not scared of them anymore. I went to the airline my sister had booked for me to confirm if there were any local planes flying. Two women were standing behind the counter talking. They looked at me briefly as I asked about the flight, then went back to their conversation as if a rough wind had blown at their neckties and they had simply put it in place. I listened for a while to their discussion about what had happened to some spray money at a wedding, and turned away. As I walked away to get an SMS credit card and call my sister, one of them said, 'If you are a stranger, there is strike and no local flights.'

That evening everyone sat before the TV. My sister's husband changed the channels every 10 or 20 minutes. He would stay longer on Channels TV which had discussants exchanging almost abusive words on issues of subsidy.

'Why is it only oil that is subsidized?'

'Look, the issue here is, everyone is in support of the subsidy. It is the timing they seem to be unhappy with and the president has said he is not happy too about the hardship the people will encounter but it is necessary. The subsidy is benefitting only the cabals and not the people.'

The cabals! Sani looked at his sister who was eating her dinner on a tray carefully balanced on her knees. The professor had talked of a cabal at the airport, now this guy was talking of cabals eating up a subsidy on oil.

'Why won't agriculture be subsidized?'

'Why won't housing be subsidized? Why won't education be subsidized so that every child in this country will go to school?'

'What of the industries that have all died off. Can't they or their products be subsidized instead of bringing in cotton and tyres? We grew rubber in the past, that's why Dunlop was here. And what of Bata? They left because we were eating all the material for leather as 'kpomo.' Why did all these companies run away to Asia? Subsidize electricity and make its supply steady. Now it's a cabal holding the people to ransom! Who is to protect the people from this cabal that seem to be a spirit or Satan himself come to live in Nigeria.'

Sani got up reluctantly to collect the food that was being handed to him by a girl that worked in the house. When he returned to his seat, his sister's husband had changed the channel. The strike was on its second day. He hoped the president would come out and say something tonight. He wanted to go home. His sister was not comfortable with the road. She said the pot holes and robbers shared a common identity. They killed innocent people and no one could do anything about it. 'Cabals of the road,' she called them.

'The cabals of the road are the ministers and directors general and supervisors responsible for the construction of roads. They tell the companies what to cost, what percentage to give them, how long to delay the work so a new contract or review would be done. So they grow fat at the expense of the roads. And people die from the deep potholes that should not be there. When I told one who is a friend that roads in Benin Repuplic were so good, eight lanes to busy ports, he asked me what the size of Benin is. This is a strange country with strange people,' my sister's husband said, changing the channel.

'Did I not hear we supply the same Benin and Ghana electricity? Why do they have steady distribution?' my sister asked. I wanted to say because they did not have a cabal but my sister continued, 'Newspaper reports said President Obasanjo gave billions for electricity. Unfortunately he was not conscious of the cabals he was putting in place to disburse the money. It went to places but electricity generation.'

'The cabals did not start with oil. It was the cabal that killed Nigeria Airways. It was the cabal that killed the Railway. The cabal put to rest farming and the booming textile industries. The cabal has dealt a deadly blow to banking. Is there any place without the cabal? We are rearing small cabals now in our homes. See our neighbour's son, five years old, removed money from the mother's purse and bought ice cream and told them I bought it for him. And no one would have known if the mother did not stop to thank me this morning. When she threatened to put peper in his eyes if he did not tell her who gave him the ice cream, he confessed he bought it and it took a while of further threats before he said it was from her purse. He must have been doing that for a while and because it is small amounts, his mother never noticed.'

'Nawao, small boy.'

'Small cabal in the making.'

'But do you blame these children? Did you listen to the talks about national honours and some recipients who were escorted in handcuffs by the EFCC? There is a man who lives big on people's contributions to the church. He is always on every program where contributions are made. He is training his little sons, one at least, to become a priest. He says a wise man would be a comfortable if not wealthy parish priest!'

I remembered the scholarship forms we had picked. Someone had told me not to worry since my mother's brother worked at ETF but Tersoo said we had a lot to border about if we had no carbal connection. Tersoo said he had some connection in the National Assembly. 'Scholarships were now only for the carbals' children,' he had said but mom had insisted I apply. She said my results were good and would take me anywhere. I did not get it even though she said I had the course and the right scores. It was obvious I needed more than ICT and good results. The cabal's idea rather than our president's seem to be taking root. Several of my friends in school were not even planning to go back home. They were sure the quality education they were getting would not fetch them good jobs at home; as such jobs were for cabal children. One of my friends said his father moved him from the Eastern University because the Vice Chancellor's wife was the deputy bursar, his children who were doing postgraduate programs were now lecturers with special allowances; a senator's daughter became a director after her National Youth Service. My school friends would rather remain where they would get jobs for their competences but for now I wanted to return home after my degree.

The strike was over and I could not wait to get home. My brother dropped me as early as 6am to catch the earliest flight I could since I had a ticket. As I hurried to catch my flight I saw a newspaper headline, 'Cabal Hijacks Jonathan's Presidency!' I stopped dead. I did not want to read the story. In spite of what people and the media said, I still held onto some hope and wanted to come back home after my studies! I did not want to loose it. I was determined to form an association I would call *The Cabal Watch*. I was sure guys were out there who, like me, felt this was not a hopeless situation. The NYSC camp would be our start off point. We would be sure to conscript people like Ralph who wanted to be the law for the very reason that they would make things work, so everyone belonged. I wondered for a while if I should appoint my Mom as an adviser. She was courageous and would not chicken out for fear of my getting into trouble. She was sure to tell them to begin with removal of the cabals in the electricity sector and I was sure to agree with her.

That night I called Wale Omotoso, Kene Okigbo, Mustafa Zungur, Bem Hagher, Wogu Saro-Wiwa and Simon Iyayi. Each promised to come with at least two well-known guys ready to go underground if necessary. I went to bed sure I'd sleep better than I had since my return home.

BABA OLUWA

A PARANOID CATHOLIC, YES, BUT Kate was often affected by other Christian denominational and Islamic views that bore any semblance to her beliefs. Those were the liberal attitudes her mother frowned at. And as Kate grew into womanhood she was convinced that her mother was unjust in her supposition that outside the orthodox churches, preachers in line with Keith Miller stood for manipulation and insensibility. That conviction led her to many adventures which culminated in that visit to Baba Oluwa.

Kate had since wondered at that naïve liberality. She would have picked holes in her attitude remembering that incident when she was but a nine year old. She had then discovered that her friend Timi`s family attended a church where communion, once a month, consisted of jollof rice, peppered chicken and fried meat and fish that weighed half a kilogram a piece. So one Sunday morning, Kate woke up earlier than the rest of the family, washed her face, put on a dress and ran off to the first mass at six. She returned, enthusing to everyone, `how refreshing. I didn`t have to sit with noisy five and six year olds because there was room for everyone.' Then she swept the compound to the delight of mama who had to contend with an untidy front yard on Sundays.

No sooner had the family left for the 7.30 O'clock mass than Kate rushed off to Timi's home as they were also leaving, carrying covered food warmers of rice and huge pieces of chicken, their share of communion. She was to later discover from conversation between Timi's mother and aunt that the large pieces of meat and chicken were an effort not to be outdone by competitors. Kate had thought the church was responsible for the communion. Any way, the service reminded her of the Bible story where Jesus fed thousands with bread and some pieces of fish. She remembered the catechism teacher saying it was the spirit of sharing that was to be emphasized in that story.

She could not remember the name of the church except that members wore long white gowns and walked barefooted. In that church Kate had sung and clapped and stamped her feet as hard as anyone else. She closed her eyes and shook her head from side to side making expressive gestures with her mouth and nose. She was only disappointed that unlike some people she couldn't fall over and thrust around. Maybe the spirit that entered those people knew she did not belong here. And at the end she was not totally disappointed because Timi and many other children of her age did not experience the power of that spirit. She later learnt from Timi that only children possessed by witches or evil spirit had a similar experience. And it lasted longer and the evil thing had to be beaten out of the child which was painful because his body had to be slapped really hard to get to the witch which kept dodging as the preacher hit at it. Kate noted that it was good to watch out for witches and avoid them. Her aunt had called one woman a witch to her face once and the woman had been very angry and jumped to slap her accuser but people had held her back. Kate could now understand the scenario.

Her brother found her out on her third visit. He was curious and determined to find out why Kate ate so little and laughed so much on the Sundays she went to mass early, cleaned the compound and was not seen until midday. He didn't believe the story about playing at the Ayeni's who also went to church. On the third occasion he was waiting when they returned. He ran home and reported to their mother. Never before or after had mama beaten her the way she did on this occasion. Kate promised never to go to any witch church as mama called them and she never did. She had wondered then how mama knew witches were beaten out of people and was sure one day they would claim there was one in Kate. She kept a firm eye on her and ensured they all went to the same mass and not until she entered the university with independence and freedom of movement did she ever step into another church.

Kate was a restless child who grew into a curious teenager. At the university she travelled around a lot, visiting friends without informing her mother. She visited her numerous out-of-town friends, attended the parties they invited her to and went to worship in their churches with their families if she spent a Sunday in their homes. She shared the cheerful life style of some families, the sad or quarrelsome nature of others. All these touched her needs, some private yearnings she couldn't fanthom. These experiences made her love and appreciate her own parents, their love, gentleness, their concern about the faith of their children. Kate was especially excited about the healing atmosphere of the convents where her mother often left her with some of the Rev. Sisters who were relations or friends.

On a trip to Lagos, in a Luxurious Bus, she sat next to a man who took an hour to pray for journey mercies. He then gave a homilectics on the loveless nature of Nigerian leaders, their bastadization and looting of the country's wealth, their greed, their encouragement of 419 and robbery. He concluded that he was preaching in the name of Olumba Olumba. Kate asked him who this person was. He said Olumba's coming was foretold in The book of Revelations, though un-named. Kate told him that all prayers began and ended with the Holy Trinity. He said that meant she was Catholic and consequently didn't know her scriptures. He believed that people in this category needed to be saved through conversion. Kate was glad when gunshots of armed Mobile policemen forced everyone down at a checkpoint. This incidence kept him in silent prayer for the rest of the journey.

Shortly after her National Youth Service, in a London bus, Kate met an Indian who told her he saw surrounding her a rich star. Kate looked at the nearest faces as if the star hung around next to her but she wanted to be sure no one was listening to this embarrassing conversation. Everyone kept a straight face looking ahead, out the window, reading a book or their eyes closed and one could not be sure if they were sleeping or listening. Londoners listened without looking at you and were good gossips. They talked about you and then smiled when you looked at them.

The Indian continued to talk about her star which included a charm that drew people to her and she needed to know how to arrest them when such an opportunity presented itsself. He told her in a strong voice that she needed to wake up, emphasizing 'wake,' as if she were sleeping and responded as if cold water was splashed on her. He said he could see many opportunities she had already missed and it made him really sad and he could not leave her in this state. He gave her an address and a lucky number and promised to guide her attain that success that may elude her if not inspired. He was a handsome man with well cut hair, not the familiar round crop. He spoke rather well for an Indian engaged in that kind of trade. Kate was sure he had lived for a long while in London.

Mother's warnings tugged at her heart about horoscopes but she was convinced this was different. After all, she had a good degree, a good job and had met a man who worshipped the very ground she walked on. Perhaps this Indian would just confirm all these. He followed her down Tottenham Road tube station and Kate began to get an uneasy feeling. She looked at him suspiciously but he only smiled and waved her on. She could feel his breath down her neck as she pushed her day ticket in the machine. Then she felt a push as he barely made his way through on her ticket! Kate removed her ticket and turned around. He was gone. She remembered her unease and her mother's warning. So long, rich star.

November is a most disagreeable month with lots of dusty harmattan winds even in Jos, known for its temperate climate. A young mother of four months, breastfeeding with the fresh memory of rains and blooming frangipanis and roses outside her windows with the recent rains would be especially sensitive as Kate was right now to the scorching sun. It was not yet a month since the rains had stopped and she was taking time getting used to the new weather. From the window she could see a green snake slide away from the yellow bushes towards the uncut bushes, past the lemon grasses. Didn't some one say snakes never went near lemon grass and that was why she had carefully placed them between the plants, hedges and against the fence? Or did the myth not apply to green snakes which they say don't bite? She looked around but could neither see the cat nor the dogs. No wonder the snake crawled out from its hiding place!

The open gutters familiar to Jos visitors were relatively clean, a legacy of the rains just ended and the rocky terrains. The streets shone with a magnificent brilliance that temporarily made the visitor forget the heat. Even the potholes, so numerous on every street, held no debris for a discriminating eye and one would readily agree that the town's real enemies were its development agents. No doubt, tax-payers could justify a certain resentment especially residents of Jenta and Tudun Wada Village, not far away from the G.R.A where Kate lived. She could see a long stretch of the Close from her window where she had strategically placed her work table and could see the goings on when she wanted to. The mango tree kept the view secret from passersby unless for those who came into the compound and stood under the tree. From that position they could look up and see Kate if the window was open and she were leaning on the wide seal outside of which she placed small potted plants.

Today Kate had taken an early bath, dressed and was sitting on her table waiting for Tolu. As she waited thoughts of Timi and the Sunday communion of her youth flashed on and off. She wondered where and what Timi was doing now. It had been over ten years now since that communion incident and they had drifted apart after going to different secondary schools and universities. She also thought of the Indian and his star. But Tolu was a childhood friend not given to frivolities. And she had told Kate it was a personal experience and she too had been introduced to Baba Oluwa by a friend who had also experienced something unique. She quickly got up from the table as Tolu slowed down at the gate. She could see the number and colour of her red Galant even though the tree obstructed the total view of the car. She hurried down, her clutch bag in hand. As they drove to Tina Junction, Tolu talked more about the miracles of Baba Oluwa and assured her it was going to be alright and she had nothing to worry about. After pointing out to her the huge parcel of land and property belonging to Baba Oluwa, Tolu dropped Kate off at her aunt's place.

Kate crossed the road, jumped a gutter and walked fast, a natural habit, to her relative's home about twenty meters away. As she walked she thought fast of how she would convince her relative of her mission, to see a man who diagonised a problem, an illness, by simply gazing into your eyes for a few minutes. She had tried in the last week not very successfully to convince herself that after all this was a man of God. So she was told.

Her friend had insisted, 'The problem with you is the lack of faith. A friend of mine went there and Baba Oluwa told her the problem – and the solution. And he didn't charge her anything. She was grateful and showed it. That's how he does his own thing. You give a token of appreciation if you wish.'

'Then I will go, but I will be at ease only when he tells me my problem.' She was strict about such things and that was why she chose to discuss with her this morning. She liked Tolu since they were kids. They shared confidences.

'Well, there is no harm in talking to him. But don't give him any information,' her aunt warned.

'Aunty, we are on one track there. Trust me.'

Kate went with her aunt's driver. She did not want to visit such places alone. As they drove into the wide yard, a man at the gate pointed to a place to the left. Several cars were parked there so the driver dropped her near the entrance and drove off to the parking area. The man again pointed to a building in the distance. Kate wondered if he were deaf or dumb. She walked past a bakery and her stomach churned a hungry hymn. The smell was enticing and she remembered she had not eaten. She built a mental block to her hunger, remembering that first morning when her mother's adopted daughter from the church now her ward, had screamed all night searching for the key to go out and dance. She had shouted at the maid for standing in her way and for looking ugly. She could again see the horror of the situation as she danced to music only she could hear and then tried to open the door against which Kate's husband leaned. Kate had watched every thing from the table, heavily pregnant. Her brother tried to stop Schola in her attempt to push the man leaning against the door, her outlet to the music she danced to once in a while.

Kate could still hear her screams with tears running down her face shouting, 'Let me out. They are calling me!' while holding firmly onto the side stool she had in her hands. Tears streamed down Kate's face even as she entered the building the man at the gate had pointed out to her. She was glad no one was in the large front room. She searched her bag for tissue, whipped her face and blew her nose. She could perceive the wonderful aroma of spices from a kitchen not too far off and she knew this building was also residential. There was a mirror in a corner and an open door that led into a wide passage. A woman of about twenty six to thirty came out of one room and went into the room directly facing the passage that led to where Kate stood. She could see the room where the lovely lady entered was a dining room with a big dining table that could sit at least ten people. Kate adjusted her blouse before the mirror and walked into the the room ahead of her, pushing the heavy curtain aside. Her eyes met several other eyes that turned almost at once at her entry. She took a place and went over her meeting again with her aunt and recalled how she had explained her mission after they had both shared tears of joy at seeing each other and how she had called for the driver and told her, 'I will wait for you for lunch.'

'Please do wait for me, Aunty. We have so much to catch up on,' Kate had replied. Kate thought over her walk into this large compound that housed three buildings. To her left was a single storey building. Rich curtains adorned the windows. The surroundings were bare of plants except a wide umbrella-shaped tree under which was parked a Santana and a Peugeot 505. In the open garage could be spotted a yellow Mercedez Benz 280. Backing the wide open entrance was a bungalow around which people could be seen in varying postures. There was a man in chains, obviously a crazed man muttering and gesticulating to some unseen subject. Kate had slowed down to give him time as he walked clumsily in his chains towards an uncompleted building to the right.

She hurried on, making her way between the bungalow and the uncompleted building where the activity was centered. In this room she was met by a man who was supposed to have urshered her into the first room before she came in here. In here she would have been met by another man who would have ushered her into this waiting room and showed her a bench opposite where two women and a man in a brown native top and black linen trousers sat. The man was in deep discussion with one of the women. Kate's thoughts were jangled by the shrill of a call bell just as she sat down. At the same time an elegant woman of about thirty-five decked in expensive lace and heavy Indian gold on her wrist, neck and ears stepped out of a door at the far end of the room.

While all eyes were turned on this ornament, the man in the brown shirt disappeared through the door the beautifully decked woman had come out. Kate sighed, counting her third position and hoping the man wouldn't take long. She had a three hour journey ahead and of course to feed her baby who hated food from a bottle. She knew her baby would spew it all out leaving the maid frustrated and unsure of what next to do.

The elegant woman was saying her good byes to the other women. Kate looked on thoughtfully…a woman is a wonderful creation indeed. Wonderful not only because she is beautiful and elegant when cultivated and well decorated in the right cloth, cosmetics and complexion but also for her abilities to carry and bear children. A woman leaves a wonderful feeling, a climax of a life's work. She was the soil into which seeds were sewn, like planting yam or some loved vegetable in the soil, nurtured with love, it germinates, all watch it grow. Like the miracle of God that she is, the miracle of life, she is the sustainer without whom life would cease. From her life bursts into existence, grows and becomes son, brother, husband and friend. Indeed God gives him sisters, women to admire, to cherish, to enjoy, to care for to maturity that she may again produce the miracles of life for him to harvest. She is that miracle in which you see beauty and the glory of God. Look at the skin, the soil…. ` Good day, sister.'

Kate turned at the rude interruption. It was the man discussing.

`Oh! Good morning,' Kate said looking at her watch. It was eleven-thirty. She was suddenly cheerful at the thought that this man was out and the woman he had been discussing with had gone in. One more, then it would be her turn.

'You look worried,' said the man.

'Yes,' Kate said, wondering what she would be doing here if she had nothing to worry about. Did he not have a problem before coming here? When people wanted to talk they said stupid things but Kate was not in the least disposed to discuss her worry about her four months old baby and her feeding habits with a total stranger.

'Not to worry. Baba Oluwa has helped many of us. But you are in good health…'

'Yes. I am not sick, thank God!'

'And you are young. You are still in school?'

'No. I have finished with school.'

Pause.

'You live with your parents?'

'No. I work.'

'But you are working. You must thank God for that.'

'Yes.'

Long pause.

Kate looked away; a determined look which stated categorically that she didn't want further discussions. The man shifted uneasily, got up and walked towards the outer door and looked out for a while, looked at Kate who starred straight ahead at an almanac, wondering why the man would not go, having done his consultation. Perhaps he thought he had seen a girl to toast. Kate felt irritated. Is there any where you went that someone was not waiting to corner you?

The shrill bell sounded again. The man returned to the room at the far corner just as the woman walked out, a sad expression on her face. Kate looked at the woman to her left, wondering whether the discussing man had forgotten something and gone for it. She listened to the women without looking at them. They whispered but Kate could hear `fast and seven'. Just then the discussing man came out and sadly motioned her in. It now dawned on Kate that the man worked here.

Kate sat on an ancient ottoman, her back against the wall. She surveyed with awe the little man sitting across her, yoga style, in an impeccable birge coloured French suit. The thick Persian rug upon which she tapped comfortably with bare feet having placed her sandals before the sign `this

is holy ground' printed atop thick soled shoes that looked
sexless. Kate briefly forgot her mission as she drank in the
distinctive role which the rich room and round leather works
had added to religion's more ancient preoccupation with
portraying values of humility. The equally distinguished
voice was an ultimate reality behind the splendor. Baba
Oluwa seemed a misnomer. A smooth faced handsome man
of thirty-five with a cultivated, authoritative bearing, he
cleared his throat aimed at placing Kate mentally into Baba's
spiritual presence. She briefly looked at his handsome face.
The shifty eyes reduced the effect. Why was she thinking of
that Indian? She tried to bring her thought to the present. Yet
this smooth face reminded her of the handsome ruggedness
of her beloved with the large eyes now generously bestowed
upon their little one. To the present! She silently scolded her
wondering thoughts. Baba had his eyes closed, resplendent
in his suit.

'Dear sister! Oh, dear sister! Indeed the devil is powerful
but God is even more so. Here you are, educated, yes, a good
job, yes, a small place of your own which will grow into
something really big if your enemies will let you be.' Pause.
Shaking of head, closed eyes. ' These are people who claim
to be your friends – good friends. Yet they are working in
dark places against you. To take the man who loves you.
His proposals of marriage are held by evil principalities each
time he meets with you. Yes if they can't have him for his
eyes are all for you, they must stop you from having him.'
Long pause, 'Day and night….

Surprise, annoyance, irritation. Kate struggled with her
emotions, finally settling on indifference. For the first time
she looked around the shrine-like consultancy. So God gave

man freedom of expression in allowing him to write His words? So the Israelites brought in a lot of their traditions into God's messages which have created confusion into the minds of people. So the picture presented at times had its selfish aspects? Yet it was buoyant and secure in tone because it still recognized the authority and kinship of God. Yet here was free expression, a sordid affair glorifying in the miseries of immorality, profiteering from poverty the negative aspects of urbanization, cashing in on personal distrust and fear of black magic. A subject that prevents many from realizing the duplicities veiled behind the veneer of respectability.

What is this room? Crowded with substantial religious relics which combined the functions of politics, religiosity with cultural and traditional affectations of worship including the Catholic rosary and Muslim chesbi in their dozens, crosses in various shapes and sizes, statues of Our Lady of Lourds, pictures of the Lord Jesus, Moses on Mount Sinai, a crescent and star and other unidentifiable carvings. A spirit of sectarianism overcomes indeed. Sanctuary tries to appeal to every religious taste. Was this a new approach to a religious reinterpretation of the new Nigerian culture? To abandon all or embrace all as represented in this half-lit room, presided over by a priest? Is this independent of traditional Biblical/Quaranic standards? Potential worshippers unsanctified by established regious canons?

A place indeed for escape, for amusement, a place that carries no richness or originality of any Christian church, a place that would empty rather than enrich spirituality…

'Sister! We can overcome these forces. Yes. Seven days of dry fast preceded by a naked bath beginning today!' He opened his eyes, wiped imaginary sweat from his smooth brow and repeated in a tired voice.

'Yes, today beginning with a naked bath I shall give.'

She could imagine her aunt asking, 'How did it go?' and Kate say to her, ' A disaster. Baba couldn`t use traditional philosophy because her names were western. His contact man met a woman, not a whimpering girl scared of her womb being closed by her jealous enemies.'

They would then tear at the drum-stick with a vengeance.

Kate remembered the hands that ever gave her bath – the tender hands of mama and the gentle one of her beloved with love. She looked at the small well-manicured fingers of Baba Oluwa, fingers that would never arouse any feelings except contempt. She thought of what to say, to hurt this naked bath giving messenger of false hopes? Then she remembered another small beautiful Irish woman whom the Nigerian road had claimed:

'Be always gracious to everyone in every situation even as the mother of Christ was gracious and pleasing to win worthily the grace of the living God!'

And Kate said simply.

'I came to see you about my schizophrenic sister now in hospital but not making much progress. A friend said you can cure her!'

He looked at her for a while and said, 'You may have seen some of them as you came in. We do not have enough space for now to take in cases of that nature until the building is complete. That will be about June next year.'

'Thank you,' Kate said, getting up, not looking at Baba Oluwa.

Kate walked past the naira-filled basket of gratification; she slipped on her sandals, glad to be away from this holy ground. She passed the contact man, fear written all over him as the bell sounded, shrill, long, incensed. He almost collided with the door. One more disaster in his assortment of wares. A Laissez-faire. His master's reputation. His job.

Kate returned to her aunt, thinking of her doe-eyed baby girl. Her father would now be rushing home for lunch and to be assured that his baby's diapers were changed. Of Indian star wonders, of Mallam's love charms and portions. Oh, those perfumes in the nose that aroused the variety seeker, commanded him to do the wearers biddings. The spirit-filled consultant who 'helped' weak, frustrated women by manipulation and cultural deformities to find some temporal happiness; women who took 'prayer' as a substitute for human resposibility.

THE OLD GIRLS' HONORARY AWARDS

IT WAS A ROUGH WORK day for Nomina but she was happy to be home with her four children. It was not often she had a full house with all four of them. She was also happy to be home with them because they rarely quarreled these days. A lot of laughter and phone calls from the girls' room and a lot of hiphop and loud sounds of the movies on the TV set in the boys' room came across to her room as she pulled off her shoes and placed them on the rack next to the handbags hanger. None of them knew she was back home until she shouted, 'Hello everyone!' Even then it was her last teenage daughter who first came out as she shouted louder to the others, 'Mom is back!'

'Welcome mom,' she smiled, hugging her.

'Hey, how was today?'

'Nothing special. Wish ASSU will call off this strike,' she said.

'Enn, let the government do what they should.' Her sister came out smiling and collected her Mom's handbag from the dressing table and hung it on the wall next to the other bags.

'Hey how was work today?' she asked Mina, now tuning to the Hug FM.

'A lot of work for me, writing reports.'

'What does the secretary do?'

'Oh she does a lot of talking when her husband or child is not sick. She is an in-law to one of the directors. But I have some good news for you.' She went back into her room and brought out an envelope which she handed to her mom. It was not opened.

'How do you know it's good news?'

'I have one myself. It's from St. Patrick's Secondary School. They are giving awards at the school to highly achieving women to encourage the students see the value of hard work.'

'Who are the winners of the awards?'

'They are keeping that up their sleeves but they have mentioned some big political kingpins and their wives who will honour the event.'

'Oh I am sure many people will turn up. I know some old girl senators, professors, even an owner of a bank, high court judges and industrialists who are old students of St. Patrick. Your former teacher is a well known dentist and I hear a lot about her Clinic.'

'I will go, mom, because I am sure you will be one of the winners. If Rotary and Women in Nigeria and National Association of women Academics et al recognize you, your old girls certainly will.'

'But who is giving the awards? I am not sure the school will do that because to them all the students are important.

That is the policy since the formation of the school over fifty years ago.'

'You are right, mom. It is an organization owned by an old student.'

Nomina did not want to disappoint her daughter. She had a workshop for Civil Defence, a few minutes drive from St. Patrick but, following the Boko Haram bombings, it had been postponed. A new date, the same as the St. Patrick's awards date, was now fixed but the organizers had not yet confirmed the venue. If it was still to be on the original venue, Nomina would be at home at the event with her daughter.

She called Halima, an old St. Patrick girl and a successful restaurant owner.

'Are you going?' she asked Nomina with surprise hinted in her voice. 'I will not go with the kind of names they have on that list. I don't want any police embarrassment with all those politicians. What is their business with St. Patrick?'

'Well, my daughter is interested and I wanted to know who and who around us here will be going so she could join you if I don't make it.'

'Now you are talking. You will be the last person I would have thought will be there. I am not going o.'

'How is business?'

'It's even better now. Two banks opened offices across the road.'

'Ah that is wonderful. Take care.'

'You too,' Halima said and cut off.

Nomina smiled and put her handset and the letter on the bed. Halima was a rather temperamental person. The present government did not favour her husband with a juicy appointment. He had also contested and lost an election. He had changed parties and though very popular in his state, the majority party contestant had beaten him to it. The loss was of cause the hand work of the majority party riggers, many had concluded, and had encouraged him to go to court but Halima had advised him not to waste his money and time. The other party was wasting money that was not theirs. He had listened to her and they were keeping a low profile. The names on that list which Halima had on her dressing table were all from the majority party, many were not even from St. Patrick but Nomina was sure they were relatives to parents or husbands of old girls which was alright in a situation of this nature.

The next morning Nomina got a reply to her mail. The original venue was confirmed for the leadership training where she was to present a paper on Group Dynamics and Equality Issues. The awards would come a day after her presentation. She called Adeola, a top radio journalist who was also a chapter president of the St. Patrick's Old Girls Association.

'I just want to know if you will be at the award.'

'Yes. In fact I am organizing a bus to take those who may wish to go from here. A few people are flying. Some are going with a bus from the presidency. You know our First Lady is an old girl, and the wife of the minister for petroleum and their friends and well wishers.'

'But I've never seen them at our meetings.'

'Yes, but we hope they will support the school with this meeting. You know the press will be there. They love things like this.'

'I hope it will not be pledges which will not be redeemed. Tell the MC small donations rather than huge pledges. I will be there but I will drive.'

'Ok, we will meet there.'

'Yes.'

Nomina was happy that Halima's view was not an all round one. For a while she was tempted to put her mind on the award and some likely contenders. She did not want to dwell on Halima's view that the awards were a politician's gift by the organizers for future deals. How many old girls of the school were politicians, any way? And the aim was to encourage the girls to see virtue in hard work, so what do politicians do that the Association will be telling girls to all aspire to be politicians. She hoped the event would put Halima to shame.

Nomina's workshop had gone better than she had expected. Her paper was well-received and the honorarium was equally good, much more than the letter inviting her had stipulated. And her friend in town would not hear of her staying in a hotel so she had been paid her hotel claims in addition to her airfare. She planned to pass these additions to the purse of the old girls' contribution to renovate the school laundry. Two years earlier they had contributed and fixed the toilets and dining hall and replaced the aluminum plates which an old girl said reminded her of her dog's plate. She hoped these politicians coming to witness their friends receive the awards would make generous contributions to extend the assembly hall which was getting smaller for the growing population.

The gate was fully manned with police and mobile policemen when Nomina arrived. She wore the Old Girls blue and white spotted uniform. The girls believed wearing a uniform was a way of putting at ease old girls who could not adorn themselves with the expensive attires common with politicians and their wives. It was also an easy way of identifying the old girls whereever they were seated. Many of them no longer looked like they were twenty, even ten years ago. One had to look big to show she was well married and belonged to the big girls clubs in the cities, some of them believed.

Nomina saw the chapter president talking to others next to a table which displayed the wrappers and T-shirts of other chapters, books written by some old girls, bags and purses made with the wrapper materials which some of the old girls were buying to compliment their outfits.

'Hello', Nomina called to this old girl and that old girl, hugging as she moved on. She could easily tell the poor, middle and rich old girls in spite of the uniformed attire. Nomina's dress was sewn by her cousin in Ivory Coast and though she had not expected it, her cousin brought her a thirty-five thousand Naira bill for a three thousand six yard wrapper to which she had added matching beads round the collar and waist and halfway down the knees. It was narrowly cut to her figure and a flare down the legs. She knew it was a good fit and she was satisfied with the looks everyone gave her as she passed by.

As she moved from one group to the other, the old girls complemented.

'Your dress is beautiful,' Amina said.

'Your dress is unique. Did you make it here?' Uwem asked.

'You will show me your tailor when we get back,' Yemi said even though Nomina thought hers looked even better.

'Hey Nomina,' shouted Elizabeth. 'Where have you been? I see you only on TV.'

'And newspaper,' Ene added. They hugged and all exclaimed, 'Here they come, let us go in.'

Nomina stopped for a while, 'Come, those are our seats.' She pointed at the far end of the hall. The front seats were reserved for invited guests. Nomina made herself comfortable on the plastic chair next to Elizabeth and Ene. The guests came in elegantly dressed. Most of them had folded the old girls uniforms on their shoulder as identification of their old girl status. Nomina was pleasantly surprised to see that the second lady, five governors' wives, two minister's wives and three ministers' of state wives as well as wives of directors and other positions not announced were old girls! Some wore the uniform heavily embroidered and their ears, chests and hands beautifully adorned with diamonds, Indian gold and beads of all expensive make and colour. St. Patrick's had indeed done well for the men of the country.

They were all seated and the National President gave her welcome address after the national anthem had been played and sung by all. She started with the introduction of the First Lady who though not an old girl was interested in what happened to girls. She was mother of all and considered it her duty to encourage all her children to read well and aspire to be like these successful women who started right where they were, obeying the rules of school and nation, obeying their parents and married good men because of what the school had inculcated in them. The president thanked the First Lady for taking off time on her busy schedule to be there with them. She listed the needs of the school and expressed her certainty that both old girls and guests would not leave without ensuring that when they came back in another year or two, 'this hall will not be the same again.' A few girls from the back shouted, 'and hostel'.

'And the school also needs a new hostel,' the president added with a smile. She hoped their 'visit will be a pleasant memory from the moment' they left. She knew 'the school will be counting cash and cheques this afternoon' because she knew 'women gave their might and not pledges like men.' Her comment about 'the plege did not apply to the men present' because she knew 'the men present were already touched by the spirit of St. Patrick's old girls' and they were 'different.'

The principal thanked the visitors and reminded them that St. Patrick's, though a Catholic school, catered for girls of all faith because its mission was not discriminatory. It saw every girl that stepped into that wall as God's children. It gave her much joy to see the girls of different faith loving and caring for each other. It was obvious that years after they had left here many were in touch and whereever they met, they saw themselves as sisters. She asked them never to forget they were old girls of St. Patrick's who were brought up to positively touch lives whereever they found themselves. She thanked them for the dining room, the toilets and laundry they had renovated in the last two years. She was happy they had plans for this hall which was built over forty years. Indeed she was happy to hear someone mention the hostel. The hostels were overcrowded which was not healthy. It is one of the reasons many girls now came in as day students and the school would want to discourage it. She was happy to see the little girls who once ran from hostel to class to dining hall to this hall were now here, 'all grown in God's love and favour.'

After the principal, now retired spoke, a few wives of so and so spoke; the second lady and then the first lady took the microphone. She was happy the president of the Association had rightly noted that she was here as a mother to all the nation's children. She was happy when her children were usefully and gainfully employed. She was sad when they did not seize opportunities as good as this and did not end up in the streets visiting violence on their fellow human beings. She could see that the school had done very well in their upbringing and hoped they would not disappoint their parents or husbands. She was sure many good men chose them because of their good behavior. It was also good they were helping their school and the young girls here now and those that will come after. They should ask their husbands who would assist them to help the school that made them the good women they married, and who had helped some of them to get good jobs and good positions. The awards they were getting today were an attestation to this upbringing. She hoped the Rev. Sisters and teachers wouldl keep up the good work.

As she spoke the impressionable teenagers watched and listened and smiled once in a while. They stood up as directed by one of the teachers and clapped loudly till their hands ached. There were murmurings of husbands among the teenagers and some smiled and whispered to those sitting next to them or behind.

Some girls came out to do some dances. They did Igbo, Yoruba and Fulani dance steps.

'Tribal dance steps,' Nomina whispered to Elizabeth.

'I hate this Igbo, Yoruba, Hausa/Fulani thing,' Elizabeth whispered.

'Well, there is little you can do now. The children are well into it before they come here. Not like us who until we left here didn't know where some of us came from, that innocence is gone,' Nomina said.

'You know that time we'd stage a play, sometimes, a Shakespearean, an Irish or even a Scottish dance with those skirts. Now we have all these Emotan, Moremi, Inikpi, Amina, Usman dan Fodio, and all we do is dance Hausa, Igbo, Yoruba out of over 360 tribes! Do you know I did not know Ibukun was Yoruba and Amina was Edo and Opubo was Rivers till years after I left school? We just loved each other but now the first question, 'from where?' Now see them trying so hard but unsuccessfully to act innocent!' Ene noted.

'The guests do not have time now to watch a play whether Emotan or Inikpi Om'Idoko. They are not even interested. The language of entertainment is money,' Elizabeth said.

'Ladies and gentlemen,' said the President of St. Patrick. 'Our aim here is to inspire our young ones here to work hard because it is only hardwork that leads humans to greatness. Okigbo was not thirty when he died but when we talk of Nigerian poets today we begin with him. Leonardo da Vinci is remembered today for his famous painting, the Mona Lisa. It has inspired painters the world over. The books we read here, I saw a student with a copy of Ojaide's The Beauty I Have Seen; the teachers all inspired us to become writers, teachers, doctors, lawyers, journalists, bankers, painters and the sweetest thing about us is we are all so composed, love a clean environment and trees around us. You know why? Look out there! It is cool no matter the weather.' She paused as everyone looked out, some standing but the line of security men blocked the windows. They sat back and she continued, 'Never mind. We are also unique. No matter how good we were in physics/chemistry/maths – we all did Biology anyway.' Everyone laughed and clapped. 'We all had some participation in the domestic sciences. Do you see why we beat the boys' schools at everything we did? And they all came rushing us to get what their own teachers couldn't give them. Now you see why we are all rounders in the office, environment, community, home! It all began here. Look at Prof. Nomina over there. She was a chapel prefect, a class prefect, the school prefect, she won writing awards and is now a professor.' Loud clapping. 'She has contributed in every project in the development of this school through the association.' More clapping. 'I hand over the microphone to the wife of the Senate President, another old girl, to handle the presentation of the awards.'

The wife of the Senate President stood up and took the microphone. He did not miss out on the protocol beginning with the First Lady and concluding with students and the press. She thanked the Old Girls for the honour but concluded, 'I am not the best to present the award so I hand over to the wife of the vice-president.' The wife of the vice-president stood up and took the microphone; she also went through the protocol and commented on her role as a House prefect which was the reason her husband chose her as a wife. He was a student in a nearby school and had met her at interschool matches and concluded firmly that, 'Our mother here, the wife of the president will present the awards. She will be assisted by the wife of the Speaker, Federal House of Representatives.' The wife of the speaker stood up and took the microphone and the list of awardees.

'Ladies and gentlemen! I want to thank the wife of the vice-president for giving me this all important assignment. We are here to reward those who through focus on academic excellence and moral upbringing are prominent Nigerians today. We are told this project is to inspire the youth on career choice, potential development and general challenges of life which they will encounter after school. Humility is your watchword. No matter your achievement without humility and tolerance you will not get anywhere.' She looked at the students at the back of the hall. They looked back unsmiling. 'You see, as a woman, you have to be humble, and tolerant to attract your husband whether you are professor or anything. It is your humility that will get you a good appointment because everybody will recommend you. This school has produced prominent Nigerians like wives of Senate President, vice-president, Minister for Petroleum, even Minister for Education, five governors here are represented by their wives, wives of Directors General here whose full names I will call as we invite them to collect their awards.'

As the names were called, Elizabeth looked at the recipients and then at Nomina who shook her head. 'I can't remember her.'

'I know that one. Her mother used to sell akara in my street,' Ene said.

'Really humble girls,' an old girl murmured from behind Nomina. She smiled and turned. It was Laila, a year younger than Nomina in school and now a permanent secretary at

'Money Ministry' as they all called the Ministry of Finance. Nomina remembered Laila, 'saucy mouth', they called her. She was far from humble and often irritated with slow, self effacing girls. Beside her was another fire-brand, Anastacia, now a Director at the Ministry of Sports. The look on her face was murderous. Nomina touched her on the knee. 'Take it easy.' She now realized Halima's annoyance.

'And finally, the wife of..........'

Laila and Anas stood up and headed for the back door. Others began to get up and follow the same direction. Nomina watched the Association's president's effort to call the house to 'order'. First lady whispered to her escort who hurried to the nearest security who spoke on his walkie talkie and in a minute, the old girls were told they could not leave until the First lady's entourage had left.

Nomina watched from her seat as the wife of the Vice-President thanked the Association for the honour and promised to communicate to the school their contributions to the hall and hostel project. The Association's president did not say it immediately but hurried to inform the P.A. that contributions were to be paid to the association and not the school. The association would disburse the money to school and compensate those who had made the event a success. Nomina could imagine her children seething with anger. The awards were for wives of those married to successful politicians.

THE BODY SHOP

It was ten years since I first visited London's Body Shop on the always busy Totenhamcourt road. I had passed it in the last several years and looked in through the door and windows at things being done to faces. I never stopped because I was not just bold often enough but was also convinced I did not need a make over. On Totenhamcourt road down Bond Street were hundrends of shops I had bought pants, skirts, dresses, blouses, night wears and cosmetics, all of which I tried on and swerved in front of mirrors to the complementary commentaries of the sales women and girls, and of course the men and boys. This assured me I certainly did not need a make over.

I was in my twenties with the loveliest skin and brightest eyes that shun gloriously into peoples faces, men and women and captured them spell bound. I didn't need a Body Shop. But I was often curious like any girl of my age to see what I would look like if I did something different and so on this day, something I could not be sure of prompted me. On this day I had a photocopier purchase which delivery was late and I had three hours to kill and as I walked past the Body

Shop, I remembered an earlier list on which I had a lip gloss but had forgotten to buy. I pushed the door and walked in to the almost genuine smiles of a woman who went beyond my request. She noted that a few natural colours, a trim to my thick beautiful eyebrows would make me unrecognizable. I sat down in the comfortable chair before that mirror which revealed more dark spots on my face than I had ever noticed.

She talked and smiled and asked questions as she swiveled me around working on my face. I watched with surprise as she pressed and squeezed out white puss from the spots on my face unto a flat transparent piece in front of me. The puss came out like worms and by the time she was through, my face was a bit sore but certainly looked cleaner. Then she trimmed the bushy brows, lined the lashes and put the deep red lipstick that has become my trade mark. Then I got a beautiful gift bag containing all the colours that had transformed me into this glamorous girl before me.

When I walked into the electronics shop for my photocopier the two men all exclaimed:

'What are you up to tonight, girl?'

And one added; 'Some lucky guy!'

I smiled coyly and they called a taxi. The Body Shop became a partner. I had their card and was into their shops around Britain and previous colonies like India and Malaysia whenever I visited.

So one afternoon I spotted the biggest sign of The Body Shop as I was driven down Sugar Creek Road where I had just had lunch and was on my way for siesta. This was my first visit to Charlotte and first sight of the Body Shop. I took note of the distances and the turns, which were few, just two corners all the four miles to Sugar Creek Road.

And the weather was great, bright sun running through the forest of trees that hid the houses on both sides of the road. No sign of rain. A good atmosphere for a walk I had missed in the last three days. I was thrilled with the thought of a long walk to the Body Shop! I did not wink in the all of one hour from 2-3 o'clock! I did not even look at the TV before me. It was all rather boring.

I had asked the friendly lady at the front desk to call me at three so I was not surprised when the phone shrilled. I picked it. 'Amina, its three,' she said and before I could say thank you, she had hung up. I heard the news at three announced and I stepped down from the bed into my newly bought knee length pants and sports shoes and waist length cotton shirt. I felt good as I walked across the road before the cars that waited for the light and me. I walked past the Shell gas station into Reagan Road wondering if Americans would buy Shell petrol if they knew what the company had done to Nigerian's Niger Delta in their exploration. I wondered what they would do if they knew that much of the oil they bought was stolen. I wondered what the workers would do if they had an idea of the wasted land where this oil came from; and that this beautiful landscaped environment which housed this Shell petrol station was a far cry from where the gas came. I was sure many Americans would hate Shell if they knew just a little of what ruins the company had made of a huge land mass of Nigeria.

I crossed the busy Sugar Creek into the quiet Reagan Road surrounded by thick forest like huge green trees. On my left were houses closer to the road with children throwing balls while the adults sat on the porches, smoking, drinking or just talking. On my right it took a while before

I noticed a few houses down the greenery surrounded by wooden fences. I got to the first 'T' junction and turned left into Hunters Road with the one thousand six hundred and thirty four houses that lined it on both sides of Hidden Valley. I entered the long road at its end and went into an Indian Shop to buy a biro and some nuts. I picked the nuts on the shelf but had to ask for the biro which was behind the cash box. The man shook his head when I asked for a biro but I could see it behind him and it dawned on me that he didn't know what a biro was. I asked for a pen and he nodded and turned round, got the pen and returned looking at me, funny. I paid for it and walked out happily.

I had walked half the hour when I began to feel pains in my toes. My new shoes were a little tight. A woman at the bus stop said something. I said hello and walked on. I did not get what she said. She spoke too fast with that chunk of Bojangle's chicken in her mouth. I was relieved of the guilt of walking away because the 112 came to a stop and she dropped what was left of the chicken into the park and, with difficulty, climbed clumsily into the bus. I walked on with a little pain in my toes, the cool air from the trees making it less painful, the smooth side walks and a few songs from birds I could not see but which took away my mind from my toes.

As another bus dropped off kids by a basketball pitch, I wondered how long I had to walk and whether I should not get on a bus for the rest of the trip. I had walked over two miles but I was not tired; but for the pain in my toes I was just warming up. A car stopped as I crossed the Hidden Forest Road. I had moved back as we would always do in Nigeria, give way to cars. But the driver did not move until

I had crossed. I waved. She waved with a wide, infectious smile.

I walked lesurely, thinking of all the pleasing things I'd do to my face and the new products I'd pick for the little lines around my eyes and huge bulges that rose high each time I had a late night. Thick eye brows were not fashionable these days and I would remember to also pick some clippers. I did not know how to use the razor blade the salons used at home. I was sure they'd have something to tighten and reduce the width of my chin.

I had made a sharp corner, all of thick bushes with no houses on either side of the road and I suddenly felt a twist of fear in my stomach. There could be some brand of militant kidnappers, Boko Haram and ritualists anywhere in the world. Suppose someone jumped out of these bushes with a knife? I stepped into the road from the side walk ad looked back to see if I'd be in the way of an oncoming car. Two cars sped by-close. I stepped back and then there, right in front of me, to my left was a police car with a police man, also watching me. My stomach relaxed and in a couple of minutes I was in front of houses amongst the trees.

I crossed Hidden Stream and came face to face with a church to my right and the medical centre to my left. It was on wide sprawlintg land and I had at first thought it was a school. I slowed down and again admired the chipped wood spread on the sides and under the trees to keep away grass and dust. Americans must have learnt to grow trees from the Tiv. But whereas the Tiv kept their trees to their compounds, Americans made forests of their streets and all undeveloped plots. While we were cutting the bush trees for firewood, they were filling their cities with trees – huge trees, beautiful green trees.

Suddenly, there was the road ahead with the speeding cars and I knew I was there. My toes hurt but I knew they would have been well rested by the time I was through at the Body Shop. I checked my bag to be sure I had not left my purse behind. I hung my bag on my left shoulder and gently robbed my neck clockwise, feeling the skin and anticipating the message I would give it shortly.

Then I was there. I saw the footpath through the hedges at the back of the large building but I preferred to walk in through the front gate so I moved on wondering what so many large vehicles including trucks would be doing in The Body Shop. But then America had space for everthing with its many wide parking spaces in every business area. There were no women around the premises. Two men talked rapidly by a truck hardly giving me more than a glance. None came out the closed doors and it suddenly dawned on me! This Body Shop was for metal bodies.

I crossed over to a 'shoes and bags' shop. My feet hurt terribly. I pulled my new sports shoes off and slapped my feet on them and wore them like slip-ons, then dragged myself to the front door of 'Shoes and Bags'. There was a note on the closed door, 'Back in 5 mins.' I turned and walked carefully down Hunters Road and stopped briefly in front of Hidden Valley Estate for a bus but there was none on this side of the road. I had a long way to walk to Reagan and then Sugar Creek.

There were so many roads in this green city; so many neat, smooth roads, not like the ones built by Berger, Dantata and Sawoe and Setraco which competed for potholes. My escort had told me the previous day when we drove round the over thirty mile ring road with so many side entrances into various parts of the city that a road had a life span. The builder must meet expectations. At home the builders cut corners after settlements and those who get settled look the other way as they head for the trade routes of Europe and America, their new access to direct cash. But when they come here, are they not impressed with the green environment? But perhaps the fear of the evil forests would not allow dreams of a beautiful green environment take root. And we have to live with driving through sand and dust in the dry seasons and mud became our companion in the wet seasons.

Many of the government people come here, stay in the 5000 dollar a day Balentine hotels and drive on the smooth roads to the banks, the benefitiaries of corruption where they must personally open their own dollar accounts. They no longer use their wives and girlfriends who have become smart and open the accounts in their own names and walk when power was lost. Here I was, walking with a little limp, on a holiday and unable to pay a S4000 medical examination which the hospitals at home did not have the equipment to do in the Federal National Hospital.

'Hello! Are you alright?' a tall thin old guy watering plants in front of his house asked.

'I am just fine,' I answered with a crack in my voice, annoyed at how easy I could be read. My face was good at betraying emotions and I was sure I could never be a good politician.

'Relax and give us a smile,' he joked.

I gave him a weak smile, thinking of my loss of cultural narrative.

'That's better,' he said and went back to his watering. I walked on tight-faced. My thoughts must have reflected on my face from the feel of the muscles on my brows. I smiled again. So much for the Body Shop.

As I limped back from the Body Shop I thought of what I would do the next day with my feet. I remembered the Walmart Store in New York where I had seen one of the many first ladies decked in diamonds and picking cheap stuff someone carried behind her. I learnt from one of the ladies that she was so generous she had to buy for a myriad of friends and relatives whenever she travelled. Been a market woman in the recent past she knew better what to buy, the woman had explained.

I had spent time in a bookshop and an hour later as I walked down towards a coffee shop, I saw my friend again. She was going to get coffee for First Lady who was getting her feet massaged. They were Chinese and they had something you could not get in the expensive hotel they were occupying. It was not the cost at all as government paid for all expenses, my friend said. It was the expertise you got from these locals and madam liked what they could do. 'You know, my madam has a very beautiful black skin but the last time we travelled to Dubai, she got excellent service and some creams from these roadside shops that give that unique glow. I am sure you can see it whenever you watch her on TV,' my friend concluded as she ordered the coffee.

That was a woman who knew how to take care of herself. If the world around us had no respect to vote for a woman, let the women fight, grooming the men they would get in those positions and rule! People who claimed to know her said. I loved this First Lady, tall, black, elegant with words that poured like water from her red lips. She loved good food, people said, and who does not, especially when it was free but 'appu' had its way. It added tons of fat in the stomach and the First Lady now surrounded by a troop of slim beautiful women made her uncomfortable. She wanted to wear the hugging skirts and blouses in fashion but they made it difficult to breathe. She watched Style on TV and admired the women most of who were not as beautiful as she was. She liked Africa Magic movies and she had complimented the new looks of Ini Edo and Mercy Johnson and her Policewoman escort had told her a few things doctors could do to get anyone look that way. At first she had laughed but all the women around her began to loose their heavy stomachs and say no to the appu and delicious soups, picking fruits and eating as if they were doing it to please her.

Our First Lady became determined to take advantage of the new scientific discoveries that beat appu to its own game. She first travelled to India where the star gazers discovered Voodoo and witches' intentions already planted in her womb. She laughed because she already had six children and would expect sympathy cards if more came along. They recommended The Doctors, a special group in London that would excise this witches' implants and so she returned home, took a six week leave, just two weeks more than government would normally give on health grounds and she flew out in a private jet which one of the most successful construction companies, a more permanent government as people referred to them, gracefully offered. They told her it was a shame her husband, the first man, could not buy an Airforce1. She had an appointment already booked with 'The Doctors' but not for their TV show, they were warned. With the huge payment in cash, they needed no warning and within days the useless Voodoo wrapped round the womb which had satisfactorily served its purpose, was removed. Of course a surgery of that nature required removal of fats and a tightening and reduction of the stomach size, which would not accept the appu no matter how much the mouth wanted. For the period she would take to recover, they assured her that she would be wise to remove the rings under her eyes as they would be all healed and sparkly by the time she walked out of the hotel recovery room to board her flight home, some cheap mags looking for patronage had claimed.

A year later here she was in New York, slim, elegant with ebony smooth skin and a tight face giving her feet a lift. And as I recalled the previous day's meeting I was determined to give my feet a treat the next day, this time at a real body shop.

THE NAKED DANCE

EKE WAS JUST ABOUT TO cross the road worried about the distance he would walk to This Day offices when the sound of explosion and fire engulfed the car in front of the building. The ground shook and instinctively he lay face down in the broken stones and blocks from a nearby building under construction. The stones and broken soil flew all over the place and he decided it was not safe to take to one's heels. He heard desperate shouts from the building where the car had just gone up in flames next to the reception. He could have been in front of the reception right now if he had gotten a nearby parking place. And because he did not want to be charged N50.00 for a half hour to park by the road side near the building, he had driven all the way towards the car wash up the street and was returning to the building when it happened. Eke kept his face on his folded arms in the dust and waited.

The sound had quietened a little and he could hear running footsteps towards him. He got up slowly and looked towards the building, then towards the footsteps. People were running towards the building and he got up too and followed. People in the building needed help and those running to the building were going to help, he thought but he was wrong. These people had no intentions of helping even those engulfed in streams of fire. A few had already run out with computers in their hands and were heading towards the nearby bushes, or streets in the distance. The crowd thickened and within a short while they were heading for shops some of which were being quickly locked up by their owners. Three young men grabbed a man who was trying to pull down a burglary proof and close his shop, shoved him aside, pushed the burglary proof up and opened the doors. Within seconds, others had joined them. Two lifted a huge TV set, tucking some items which Eke could not see clearly in their pockets.

Eke looked around helplessly. There was no sign of police men. A taxi stopped near Eke and the driver and two men came out, opened the booth and ran towards a building materials shop. They returned shortly with buckets of paint which they dumped into the booth, got into the car and drove off. Eke saw two other men loading chandeliers in a Toyota pickup from another shop. He looked up at a window on the first floor where a woman was trying to jump. Eke ran over and pulled a ladder he had seen against a wall next to the building. He dragged it and placed it below the window and the woman stepped down, her flared dress folded on her chest leaving her lower part exposed. Eke helped her down.

'The staircase has collapsed and there are people in the next room,' she said and then began to shout.

'Come to cash office o! There is a ladder! Amos.'

'Come to cash office,' and before long, two people were looking down the ladder.

'Drop that dispenser, you thief,' the woman shouted at a man who had just come out of a door with a dispenser, followed by another with a chair.

'You no tank God say you don commot. Not you get am', the man with the chair said as he walked up the road, greeting another who was carrying a park of tiles, followed by one with a door which had come loose by the explosion.

Eke looked at them briefly and up the road. People were running but he could not see any security or fireman. He ran to the side of the building with the ladder to the cries for help. He saw two men dragging out a refrigerator. They had already placed a wall cabinet which the woman above on the window seal was begging them to move it near where she could drop on. She was screaming at them when Eke brought the ladder. She first dropped her wrapper which was in her hand, then stepped down hurriedly.

'Take your time', Eke called out, holding the ladder to the wall. The two men came out again, one with a desktop and the other with a water dispenser. The woman charged at the one with the computer and it fell down. The man kicked her in the stomach and she doubled over, holding her waist.

'Everyday for Una. Today na we', he said, looking at Eke scornfully, as he made a call.

'Where you dey', he asked someone on his mobile, listened for a while, then said, 'Be fast and bring the pickup, let's remove these things before these police mugus come.'

He looked at Eke and pointed to another window. A man rather fat was waving frantically. Eke took the ladder to the window and placed it against the wall. Across the road a huge crowd looked on. Most focused on some corpses that lay in varying positions and ignored the looters and a few like Eke helping those stranded in the building. A man ran over to Eke and shouted at the fat man who was trying one leg after the other, unsure of which to set on the ladder.

'What are you doing? Is it not a woman just came down from the other window or you think this man has nothing to do?'

'He is too fat,' Eke said

'So what? Other people need this thing. If you don't come down in the next one minute I am taking this ladder to someone now!' He turned to Eke, 'You see the looting? I went to the police station before coming back here. Where are they?' As he spoke the fire men drove in, people slowed down making way for them.

'I hope they have water', Eke said. The man who had introduced himself as Atimga hissed at the mention of water and turned to the ladder. The fat man was on the last two steps and Atimga pulled him off. The man fell heavily on his buttocks.

Atimga grabbed the ladder and Eke followed. The fire men were dragging hoses from their tank and some standers-by offered to help. Atimga and Eke hurried to the side of the building with less smoke and fire. They agreed anyone on the inside would be on that side if the centre was still together. As they hurried off Atimga saw a man with a carton trying to escape by a side door. He swung the ladder to his right and returned it fast and hard on the man's back sending him flat on his face. Eke picked the carton and put it on the floor inside the room the man had just come out.

Eke looked side ways at the man beside him. He had no difficulty understanding why this man, obviously strong, was not a looter. From his appearance he was clean and polished and all the while spared no one while helping in this situation where the inefficiency of the state could not sufficiently curtail the rogues. As he moved along giving a hand here, shouting at someone there, he told Eke an experience he had encounted. Just two days earlier he was at a scene where a coca cola truck had smashed into a building. Fortunately it was 11am and children were at school and men and women at work. He was ashamed to see cars stop and load their boots with bottles of soft drinks. Once he established the safety of the driver and his mate, he had driven off. Eke's mind was on his uncle's recent appointment at the Airspace Management Authority as an Assistant General Manager. He was the 255th on the row and he was to meet Senator Akpan this morning. The rumour was already making the round that Senator Akpan was in Israel with an erectile dysfunction which the doctors were certain was a symptom to a serious heart disease. His uncle was a close confidant of Senator Akpan and in the last two years he had brought him several preparations from the village to alley his worries over the ED.

Just last year, his uncle had visited a babalawo who needed a man's spare part to prepare a once and for all treatment for Senator Akpan. He had called Eke and in a few words had asked Eke to show appreciation for all he had done for him in this little matter. He reminded Eke of how he had insisted on keeping him and sending him to school from secondary school to the university when his mother, who was his sister, had died and his father had married a young girl who didn't want him in the house. Eke remembered too well. He was sent to the village but his uncle had come home for a visit, had seen that Eke was worth two paid servants and took him to the city. Eke knew the Madam did not like him and quarreled with her husband that night to his hearing. But Eke soon won her over. He kept her house clean, her shoes polished, and her bath sink sparkling and ensured that dust did not settle on the black leather chairs, not even in the harmattan. Whenever she sent him to buy anything he would give her the change even if it was one kobo. Her son who was known for not concentrating on his school work, for always failing his math homework was now excelling to the surprise of the teacher who mentioned it to his mother and father. He was also becoming more responsible and they knew Eke was the source of the new changes.

Madam it was who asked his uncle to transfer Eke from the public school to St. Gregory where their two children were and to the university to keep an eye on them and their friends who may happen to be in any cult. After graduation, his uncle got him a job as a P.A to a close political associate who needed a trustworthy assistant. The job came with a government allocated house. So when his uncle asked him to appreciate, he nodded and quietly retreated.

Eke spent all night thinking of this request, to get a man's penis for Senator Akpan's medicine. By 7:10 when his uncle came knocking at his door, he was dressed. His uncle answered his greeting as usual with a fixed grin and asked after his health as he had often done. But he did not come into the wide open door. He handed Eke a leather bag, the types one was given at conferences and workshops and said he had to hurry to the office. Eke watched him walk back to the car. His driver gently closed the door, got into his seat and drove off. Eke went back into his sitting room and dropped the bag on the chair. He knew what it was – money for the work he had been assigned to do. His uncle didn't ask if he knew anyone who would get the supply. He expected him to get it.

At 10 am Eke was at the General Hospital to see Okey, a colleague's relative who worked in the morgue. The colleague often jokingly said things about the nature of his relation's job. He supervised the cleaning and dressing of corpses after their embalmment. He had once said a girl in his office had the kind of legs that as soon as she entered a room, his 'guy' would begin to nod until it was impossible to get up from his seat and he concluded, 'like that of the corpses which my relative Okey would often forcefully crack down to keep from standing and disfiguring the pants put on them.'

Eke found Okey easily and took him aside for a chat. He introduced himself as James from Kaduna and briefly told Okey his mission. At first Okey said he was a Christian and could not do such a thing. He reminded Eke that it had to be fresh to some extent and he could loose his job if such a thing got out. Eke opened his brief case and showed him wads of five hundred naira bills, and then gave him one bundle of fifty thousand and thanked him for listening to him. He closed the bag clumsily giving Okey a full view of the money and said slowly in the process that he was on his way to Kaduna where he lived and was sure to find someone more cooperative. Okey waited for a while as if in thought, then said slowly, 'Let me ask the person on duty now. Give me one hour, and then call me with this number'.

He scribbled some figures on a piece of paper he picked on the ground where they stood and handed the rough piece of paper to Eke.

'In an hour then, remember I am on my way to Kaduna,' Eke said, walking slowly to his car, thinking. How did Okey know the spare part had to be fresh? That had not even occurred to him. Last night his thoughts were engaged with the Chairman of the Presidential Committee on the Rationalization and Restructuring of Federal Government Parastatals Commissions and Agencies' submission of the committee's report. He could not understand the Assembly's difficulty with the report which spelt out clearly the reasons behind the high cost of governance in the country. Everyone knew that the over-bloated bureaucracy, the over-lap and duplication of functions of Federal Agencies, Parastatals and Commissions were of no use to work and budget and over all development. But that did not seem to bother them. His friend had told him the other day of girls sent to offices who knew nothing about the jobs they were sent to do. They just sat and painted their faces and nails in the office and ate popcorn or meatpies and drank diet coke until about mid day when they began to give one reason after another and leave.

Eke ran into a hold up and slowed down. It was a checkpoint with soldiers searching for Boko Haram bombs. On the other side of the road were policemen asking for driving licenses and 'particulars.' A hawker noted that the police were checking for a missing vehicle. Eke wondered if the vehicle had no brand. And just when he was at the Jabi Park, a Road Safety operative in uniform flagged him down.

'Your driving license, please,' Eke handed it over.

'Your papers.' Eke again handed over the photocopies he carried with him in the car.

'Open your boot, please.' He got out and opened the boot. The man examined the car carefully and then handed over his driving license and the papers. Meanwhile cars passed by.

Eke drove on, his thoughts on the anger of representatives of Universal Basic Education Commission, the Nomadic Education Commission and the National Commission for Mass Literacy, Adult and Non-Formal Education over the committee's suggestion that they were doing the same work and needed to be merged. All had stood up, their gowns flowing off their shoulders as they shouted down a member of the committee who had said that their performance was poor and they had challenges that could be addressed more effectively if they operated as one agency. One of the executives stepped out in anger, his dress got hooked on the arm of a seat and he stumbled to his knees but was quickly brought to his feet by those close by. Someone had suggested that if the agencies remained, they were not to receive government funding. They should be self-funding or commercialized. The man who had stumbled shook with anger when he was asked to return to his seat. Eke had felt sorry for the man. Like his compatriots, their appointments were based on government funding which they drained into their private accounts. They were not cut out for commercialization. Eke called his colleague. He would be late.

He parked by Mr. Biggs and walked over to a pay phone dealer, looking away as he collected the Nokia handset. He had spent almost an hour and a half in traffic for less than a ten kilometer drive. Opposite him were hundreds of cars in front of a petrol station waiting for their turn while the attendants were busy selling to the blackmarket dealers in jerry cans. The cars had now formed two lines taking the lane of oncoming cars. He felt lucky he could easily drive out where he was when through with his call. He called Okey's number and said,

'Okey this is James. It's over an hour. The traffic is heavy.' He had introduced himself to Okey as James.

'Yes. The man says some accident victims just in from Lokoja road. In fact they are removing them now and one is very bad, all broken and I think no problem,' Okey said.

'What are you expecting?' Eke asked.

'Look you can give me what you like.' Okey had received more than some would offer, he reasoned.

'I will wait in the car park exactly in two hours from now. Just walk over to the car.' Eke said

'Fine. Ok, Mr. James,' Okey nodded as if Eke could see him. He was sure the man's name was not James but that did not concern him.

Eke handed over to Okey a black shopping bag containing 200k and told him what was in it as Okey handed him another black shopping bag doubly packed. None said a word as the other turned and walked back to the morgue while the other wound up and drove off. His uncle had given him 500k. He had spent 250k and he took the balance and the spare part back to him. His uncle was obviously pleased with the expression on his face, a change from his usual fixed smile. He waved away the bag with the money. 'That was fast,' he said.

And now, two years later, Senator Akpan who had been appointed a board director after his tenure as a senator with Eke's uncle as his deputy, was in Israel dying of atherosclerosis. His uncles' medicines had not prevented the hardening of his arteries. Not even the penis mendicants had stopped the chunks of plague breaking off into his blood stream and blocking flow of blood to his brain.

His uncle had just returned from Israel. The Senator's situation was terminal and Eke's uncle had to see someone, some connection, to get him replace his dying friend. It was preparatory to his bid to replace his friend that he had asked Eke to drop some hints at This Day Newspaper and some other media houses extolling his suitability for that position with his wealth of experience. Eke was on his way, for this all important assignment, to launder his uncle's name, let people know his loyalty, his love and dedication to his job and to Senator Akpan when the bomb exploded. The sheet of typed paper was there in his pocket as he touched it once in a while to reassure himself it was still there. As he ran around with Atimga helping victims, a question crossed his mind several times – would anyone have bothered about him if he had fallen victim here? What would his uncle have done if he were lying there under the rubble?

Eke's situation reminded him once again of his friend Bipi who had joined his uncle's Church of All Seasons to head the Kidnap committee popularly called Youth Wing. They had at first kidnapped foreigners but with the tight security around foreign employees, they had turned their attention on wealthy church members and politicians. They would kidnap the victim, drive him around while one of them in another town called his family members and fixed the ramsom and where it could be paid. They had made a lot of money and opened churches in eight towns. Bipi was attracted to one of the church members, a commissioner who wanted him as an aid. His uncle released him completely from Church duties when the commissioner became deputy governor and asked him to contest the councellor election and then local government chairman. Eke was shocked when the news of Bipi's kidnap and murder made headlines. The gang was arrested and its leader turned out to be the church leader's son. He confessed that the target was the deputy governor who without their knowledge was represented by Bipi who was not known by the front boys who had shot wildly, killed four people including two policemen. They had shot Bipi when it became obvious he knew them all. In fact the young man confessed that his father had asked them to finish Bipi.

Eke shook his head in despare as he helped evacuate those trapped in the burning building. He felt tired. He was determined to start a new life without his uncle. He too had paid his debt.

GARMENT OF SHAME

ISOKAN MOVED AROUND THE HALL distributing fliers and posters to conference participants from different universities, greeting each with the word, 'shallon' as she was wont to do these days. As she walked around, she avoided eye contact with Ave who sat on the first seat of the second row watching things in her calm and innocent posture Isokan so much hated. It hurt her to see Ave who was at least six years older than her with four grown children look so much younger. But she consoled herself with the presence of her three children who ran over side stools, jumped on the center table and on the heavily stuffed chairs that crowded her sitting room. She counted herself very lucky. Many of the senior girls who married as late as she did were not this lucky. One was contantly losing pregnancies since she got married and the other could not have any at all and was reluctant to adopt. And she had had her fill of men some who barely tolerated her but was sure Ave was having affairs with a few of the men she had given up since she became born again.

Ave looked around her at other participants. She was looking for a familiar face she could relate with. She was bored with the man beside her trying so hard to get aquainted. Then she saw Afiong and quickly looked away. How would Afiong and Isokan react if they came face to face? Ave remembered when she first joined the institute and was nursing her last daughter who was now in secondary school. The two girls had clashed over the director of the Research and Documentation. Dr. Egurube had dated Afiong before Isokan joined the Institute and within a week, she had accompanied him on a trip. Afiong got the gist of it from her driver and was ready when the two returned. Afiong who never wasted time on such matters walked up to Isokan in front of the library and said in a soft tone, 'No matter how much you... 'and she gave a few descriptions and looked in Isokan's face. I advise you to look elsewhere if you want to be here for long. Ask Friska what I do to people who trespass.' The discriptions fit. It showed that Afiong was a familiar guest.

There were stories of Afiong and the Chief Executive and a baby but even as Isokan could understand the situation she had herself to worry about. Love your neighbor as yourself to her meant love yourself first before you could contemplate loving another. She was determined to move fast and get to the top before marriage and its restrictions. She had been on the job now for fifteen years. She had friends who had rushed into marriages with the belief their husbands would see them through school and get good jobs for them. Many had remained where they were. Several had walked, babies in tow. Many were pathetic complaining, hoping things would turn around. She did not want to find herself in any of these situations.

Her mother had been a cleaner in Osobo University. She had faced her world with craft and determination. She had quickly acquired native wisdom from her mother and her illiterate siblings. She stood up to the priviledged students who had a lot of money to spend on clothes and good food. She was lucky to have a mother who worked and lived close to the campus, just a walking distance. She rarely had to take a taxi. She did not have the money and it was just alright that she could eat whatever she cooked at home before going to the campus. She also knew the randy staff who were also ready to spend money. She knew the Lotharios in the management cader who gave her some money for up keep and ones in town who took care of her siblings school fees leaving her mother with the responsibility of house keep.

Living on campus also gave her a lot of advantages. She knew early about infections and birth control and she knew when to insist on a condom. Her mother did not restrict her movements; indeed she shielded her from gossiping neighbors and had a ready excuse for her when ever busy bodies told her mother anything about her movements. One day one neighbor had come to her mother and said

'I saw Isokan at 'Ever Ready Hotel'yesterday with….'and before the woman would finish, she replied, 'I have a relation who works there. I sent her. And what were you doing there?'

'I went to deliver plantain; the woman replied tersely and walked away. She knew what she saw and was now sure as neighbors were saying mama Isokan was encouraging her daughter to do the Italy business.

Many of Isokan's secondary school mates had left Nigeria and were building houses for their families. Isokan was thankful that her mother had seen the value of a

University education and had worked hard to start her off. It was her duty now to help her mother with her siblings so that they could later put heads together and build her a befitting house.

Isokan had joined the civil service with a degree and ahead of many colleagues. Then she registered for a part-time masters program and then a Ph.D. few women had a Ph.D in the civil service which was a great attraction for the men she worked with and each of them had a purpose and something to offer her progression.

Egumbe had not just being the minister of state; he was also very close to the President. He also was separated from a wife who suffered a mental problem and then disappeared. When she asked him what would happen if she someday appeared, he had replied with such confidence she was sure he knew something about the woman's disappearance. He had first replied, 'after eight years?' Then had said, 'I doubt if she will ever come back. You know how they just keep going and going when they are in such a condition. They never return.' He had then told her that he wanted to keep her and she had believed him. She was sure it was time to settle and have a family of her own.

It came as a surprise one afternoon when a woman from personnel came to seek her advice on a problem she had with Affiong. She was sure only Isokan could step in on her behalf as Affiong was 'very close to the minister of state and anything could happen to her job.'

'What do you mean?' Isokan had asked,

'Ah madam Doctor, I don't know but everybody talks about it. One time she was away for almost a year for 'a job outside' but some said she had a baby for him that time and that the baby is with her mother.'

'Ok. I will see what I can do.'

She had talked to Affiong and then the minister and things had sorted out positively in the woman's favour. Isokan had got substantial information from both Affiong and the minister of state.

Isokan had pushed the relationship which led to their trip abroad. She could have handled Affiong if the minister of state was supportive but from the body language he was not. It was obvious he had a softer spot for the other woman. Isokan wasted no time in asking for a transfer to a directorship that was open at the Institute for Peace. The minister who saw this as a better resolution to the pending conflict got it done and Isokan moved. She quickly re-ignited a relationship she had put aside for the minister and within seven months they had conducted a quiet marriage with a few colleagues and relatives in attendance.

Isokan joined her husband's church and got born again. Few of them knew her and her doctoral title not only crowned her but her husband, a single degree holder with a Ph.d wife. Though his family frowned at this relationship, he was determined to give his wife what she could not give herself, a good house and children. Though not enterprising, she had ideas he could use. She also had useful contacts from previous relationships he was sure she would not go back to, he believed.

Isokan let those who had known her previous life style know that she was no longer the same. She went on all night vigils, fellowships and retreats. She went late for meetings and left early for vigils. She took her children to meetings and cocktails and spent time taking them to the toilet and visiting a corner or nearby room where she would leave them. She learnt to pray in tongues and kept her distance from people like Ruth and Ave. she believed because they were catholics and hypocrites they had hidden their life style and people saw them as more responsible than her but she knew better. She was sure that Ave was seeing two men she had dated. One of them was a life time acquaintance, she had believed but was now openly showing greater interest in Ave's NGO. She was sure it had nothing to do with career.

She had found an opportunity to put Ave down hoping Ave would get angry and let things out but she had gently asked Isokan to calm down! She had reminded her of their responsibility as mothers! She had said she was sure Isokan was upset about something before coming to the office that morning and hoped the Holy Spirit would sort out the situation!

Ave had an NGO on Peace Research and was invited to almost every event at the institute. She had at first dropped her name from one of the institute's programmes but at the last minute the Executive Secretary had called her attention to it. He went ahead and called her. She was sure Ave had something going with the ES. Hers was not the best organization. Why did he insist, in fact ensure that she was at every event, sometimes with sponsorship. The previous year, Ave had organized a programme for the youth focusing on touts and girls who were in town without jobs or place of residence. The ES had asked the directors to encourage everyone to attend! It turned out to be a who was who event and the way she moved from one to the other with feigned humility, Isokan was sure she had a relationship with most of the people. And to her amazement the ES seemed not to notice. That night she thanked God for been born again and not a hypocrite like Ave and Ruth, and indeed Affiong who was now married to their former boss who was now a minister of Agriculture. The boy she had hidden with her mother was now public and looked very much like the father whom she was sure had killed his first wife. She thanked God for her husband and children. She was wise to have gone back to him, she thought. He was now doing so well and those women who had looked down on her could not boast of cars or a home to compete with hers. Perhaps in the next few months she would organize a thanksgiving and invite them! Yes, she would show them how far she had gone.

With that thought in mind, she walked over to where Ave and Ruth sat and shouted a genral greeting and personally gave them a flier to mark the twentieth anniversary of the institute.

THE DRIVER

HENRY WATCHED THE CROWD, A little smile on his face. Here were some people who in the recent past never considered his greetings worth answering, walking up to shake his hand with wide smiles on their faces with pretended respect. At the far corner in the second row of the high table sat Bamuza who avoided his gaze each time he turned that way. An hour earlier he had walked the whole length of the four rows greeting those who had come to grace the reception after the registry. Bamuza had no choice but to take his hand in greeting with a forced smile. He could not swallow the fact that his late brother's wife was not just sharing bed with the same brother's driver and confidant but was now married to him. It was hard to accept this situation. It would have been easier if his brother's wife were just any woman you could push around, or from a poor family from some remote village without connections, Bamuza thought bitterly. Henry knew all these because servants from his home talked to servants in Bamuza's home and reported to his sister who had a playful disposition and related confidentially with servants in his home. With regards to the rumours he got from his sister, he took precautionary steps in his marriage. Though Angela was a staunch born again Christian, he had convinced her to accept the registry and then invite her pastor and members of his congregation to the reception. If she insisted, they could get the wedding blessed in the church at some later time.

Henry's sister Grace bustled around in her 'family uniform' especially proud that she could wear the same expensive lace and judge material as Mrs. Bamuza who sat at the high table with that haughty frown. Her expensive jewelry did not make her look better than she who was serving the big people, Grace thought. With her new job at her brother and Madam's hotel she will soon begin to wear expensive jewelry too. After all the gold madam gave her for this occasion could compete with those of the other big women and Grace believed her trim, tall figure was something the plump well off women definitely envied.

She looked towards her husband and was pleased with his clean and fresh appearance. He had changed in the last three years since her brother and madam put him in charge of developing their properties. He was the one buying and supplying building materials to the builders and ensuring that no fake materials were used on the sites. From working on other people's buildings where he sometimes went for weeks without a job, he was now foreman and supervisor. They now had a house of their own even if not as big and elegant as that of the Bamuza's. Her husband said they would build a block of flats of a two story building in the same compound and rent them out. She was sure things would even be better with her brother now married to madam, she mused as she served the food first to her brother, then madam. She spoke to her friends to attend to Bamuza, his wife and those around him.

Angela gave Grace her wide, infectious, trade mark smile and Grace almost fell over the table with plates in her hands. She steadied her feet and kept her eyes on madam as if afraid to look away as that may not be polite but she could see her brother's pokered lips in the corner of her eye. He had done well for himself. She always knew he would do well as their mother had always told him to their hearing and when he could not continue with his education after their father died his mother never stopped believing that he was cut out for great things. When Grace disagreed with his plan to marry his childhood friend who had gotten NCE at the College of Education, he told her she was content with his ability to go beyond what he then had at hand. And they were happy, he a driver, she a teacher until he lost her to delivery of their second child who survived her.

Grace was then breast feeding her daughter who was three weeks older. She took on the boy and nursed them both, her mother helping out when she was not in the market with the first boy. Mother had tried to convince Henry to get a wife but he had been silent. Grace believed he wanted an educated girl like his late wife or too sad to live with another woman so soon after her death. His son Ofoma called her mama even though they were now ten and eight and living with him and their new mother whom they called mummy. Madam's four children were older but took so naturally to her brother's children. Grace's heart lept with joy the few times she heard them introduce Ofoma and Praise as their brother and sister. They did that even more frequently when they travelled to Paris, Grace in tow to help with the family who seemed to need little of her help. She had learnt a lot of French words on that trip on outings with the children. Her brother had enrolled in a school where you could speak French in ten days. Madam was a bilinqual secretary and had worked with a company where she made good money and helped her late husband's business bloom, many had told her even though the husband's relatives never wanted to accept that. She had a bank account in Paris too. Grace could see from the cheque book and ATM card with her name on it.

The trip to Paris was especially exciting with the moving stair cases that rolled you up and down. Then there was the train that took them from one terminal to the other to collect their baggage. She felt sorry that with so many big government people and money and land at home, they could not build large airports with trains and big baggage collection points. Everything was so tight and crowded at the few airports she had travelled with Madam back home and Grace wondered why they could not improve on the size of these airports when they built larger houses every day.

More people were arriving to celebrate with Madam and her brother and Grace moved over to serve her brother with a wide smile on her face. As she put a silver glass before him, Henry whispered to her. He did not look up and you had to be observant to notice his lips that barely moved. But Grace got the message clearly and hurried with what she had to do and headed for a mobile toilet from which she slipped away to the parking lot. Yes she could now drive and had a Toyota Corrolla of her own, registered in her own name. Someone had sent Henry a text that Obare had left the event for the house and was suspicious of his intentions. Henry wanted her to check on the house.

Holding her wrapper up the knee to enable her move faster, she hurried off to the car, kicked and in haste, reversed into a Kia. No serious damage apart from a little dent and fortunately no one was watching to waste her time. She drove off and had to slow down some muddy patches of road upon which Mr. Ibu, the Nollywood star frowned down the huge poster on cars and passers by. Grace drove past the murky environment looking at the door posts of shops along the pot-holed roads where she once traded in charcoal and second hand frocks and under wear. The mechanic 'shops' looked desolate as they often were but the charcoal place was busier and a woman in short pants on leggings pricing loudly was attracting attention. A police woman in uniform looked on with little interest. She looked out of place in a new well ironed blue top and a well made up face. She was sitting on a bench in one of the make shift stalls of umbrella roofs. She could be mistaken for one waiting for someone rather than overseeing the area but would come alive with a slight mistake that needed settling, Grace thought as she turned into the tarred and neat road that led to her brother's recedence.

She saw the pickup parked in front of the gate outside the large storey building. The security man had cleverly refused to open the gate 'to anyone'as instructed on his mobile phone, Grace noted as she drove past the house and parked round a bend where she would not attract attention. She changed into a flat slip on and hurried to the house. She went in through the side door and saw Okon looking at the door through which the man had just gone into the house.

'Do not make a noise,' Grace whispered and Okon turned to look at her with great relief on his face.

'I go to the back when he horn an after some time e come down come enter for di small door an don near the front door before I greet. E no even answer me just hurry inside,' he explained as if the fault lay with him.

'No worry, leave the door open. I may come before or after him but no say anything.'

'Alright ma.'

Grace moved to the door which had been left open, stood by the side and peeped, then went in. She stood by the round table in the foyer and listened. She heard Obare's voice and wondered who he was talking to. She went into the second door that led into the sitting room and moved to the stair case and peeped again and there was Obare, black plastic bag in one hand from which he deeped and sprayed an ash coloured powder on the stairs. She watched him as he turned left still spraying the powder towards Henry and madam's rooms. Grace knew the doors were locked so he would spray that stuff in front of the doors as he had done on the stair case and the passage way calling Henry's name intermittently. His job was a simple one and it could simply be erased, Grace thought as she hurried out and back to her car. As she walked out of the side door at the gate, she told Okon to get water and wash the stair case as far as oga's doors and mop thoroughly as soon as Obare was out of sight. Okon shook his head in understanding.

Grace waited until Obare drove away. She heard him telling Okon he had come to collect his phone which he had left in the chair he sat on earlier that morning and had seized the opportunity to use the toilet. He warned Okon never to leave his duty post without locking the gate otherwise he would tell his brother to look for another security man. Okon nodded vigorously and locked the door. He hurried off to attend to the instructions Aunty Grace had given him. He knew the seriousness of his assignment. He had to get every bit of that powder washed away so that the medicine would have no effect on oga for whom it was intended, he thought. Grace returned to the reception and was happy to see that her space was left unoccupied. She reversed carefully and parked, came out and inspected the Kia. She got a face towel from the box in the passenger hand rest, poured water from a bottle in her car and returned to the Kia. She rubbed off the colour it had stained her bonnet and then cleaned round the damage on the Kia. It was a scratch that would not be noticed immediately, she observed and went into the crowded arena. She took some bottles of wine and walked over to the high table. She refilled her brother's glass and whispered to him. He warned her not to mention the incident to his wife. Grace nodded and went to take her position of directing the helpers.

Henry picked his blackberry from the table and called Okon. 'Yes sir. I am doing the work Aunty gave me to clean.'

'Good and what will you do as you do the work?'

'Call his name and cancel and when I finish I go put that holy water wey pastor give madam.'

'Very good,' he said, got up and took his wife by the hand and stepped onto the dance floor. The crowed roared, cheering, clapping, running to spray one thousand naira notes on them as they danced to 2face's *You are my African Queen*.

Printed in the United States
By Bookmasters